SHAKING
THE
MONEY TREE

SHAKING THE MONEY TREE

Mary Pat Mullaney

AN
APPLE
PAPERBACK

SCHOLASTIC INC.
New York Toronto London Auckland Sydney

ISBN 0-590-43150-1

12 11 10 9 8 7 6 5 4   1 2 3 4 5 6/9

Printed in the U.S.A.   40

First Scholastic printing, September 1991

To Catherine Margaret Julia Dillon,
mentor of my childhood —
fairy godmother, too

SHAKING THE MONEY TREE

1

If they didn't come soon, I was going to jump out of my skin. Dad and Gramps had left for town this morning at seven o'clock, and here it was past suppertime. I had been up in my tree for over an hour, just watching the road and waiting.

I hate waiting around. Mom calls it a nervous stomach. My best friend, Janis Barlow, tells everyone to stay away from Kate Gormley when they're giving out report cards. Mom and Janis are both too polite to come right out and say it. But I will. I throw up when I'm nervous. That's just the way it is.

But I would just as soon be nervous up here in my big oak tree as anywhere. It's the oldest tree on our farm, and it stands on a hill that overlooks the whole countryside. On a clear day like today, I could see all the way down Five-Mile Road to our church, past the creek, and across the bridge to my schoolhouse.

I had my whittling knife out and the piece of cedarwood I was working on. I was making a frog. I had already carved his head, neck, and the two front legs.

Whittling always helped when I was nervous. I have been whittling for a long time — almost half my life, come to think of it. Gramps had given me my first knife when I was five years old, and I am ten now. He had taught me how to carve the very day I turned five. The things I had whittled at first, like the pine clothespins I made for Mom when I was seven, looked pretty dumb to me now. Every time I saw them on our clothesline, I wanted to dig a hole and crawl in.

"Get rid of those things," I told Mom. "They look like twin slugs with hats on."

"Never!" she said. "Your clothespins are better than any store-bought ones."

She was dead wrong, of course, but I couldn't say that to my mom.

I looked at the little pile of wood shavings that had fallen on the branch I was straddling. I held my cedar frog at arm's length and checked him over. His eyes, his nose, his mouth — they were all there, right where they should be. He was just about finished, and he looked pretty good, even if I did say so myself. I blew the shavings off the branch and watched them float down to the ground. Then I looked past them and down along Five-Mile Road for the hundredth time. Still nothing. What could be taking so long?

"Important family business, Kitten." That's what Dad had said when they had left for the bank in downtown Groverville this morning.

The only important business we have is our farm. Dad and Gramps own it and work it together; that and the twenty-acre strip adjoining our land that we bought last January.

Last spring we got hit hard. It was the worst drought that anybody had ever lived through. We lost most of our crops and had to fork out more money to replant. Now the payment on the new land was about due. That's the reason Dad and Gramps went to the Groverville Citizens' Bank — to see if we could get more time to make the loan payment.

If the bank said no, then we could lose the new strip of land and part of our farm, for sure. I had heard Mom and Dad talking about it the other night when they thought I was asleep.

There was a cloud of dust on the horizon, getting bigger and bigger. Then I heard our truck. No mistaking that rattle . . . like a pig with hiccups. Finally, the dust lifted, and I could see our green pickup.

I closed my knife. Gramps always said you have to be careful with a knife, even when you are in a hurry. I slipped it and the frog into the back pocket of my jeans, climbed down from the oak tree, and rushed to meet the pickup truck.

Dad pulled up alongside the house. Gramps got out first. Then Dad. I took one good look at both of them, and I swallowed hard. I had never in my life seen looks on their faces like what I was seeing at that very moment. Just standing there staring at Gramps and Dad, I practically stopped breathing, until Dad put his arm around my shoulder and led me toward the house. Gramps followed with his head down and his shoulders sagging.

"Come on, Kitten," Dad said softly, "we've got some news to tell your mom and grandmother. Let's go in the house and get it over with."

Later that night when I sank down deep in my featherbed and watched the moon light up the hayfield, it all hit me, like a punch in the stomach. Dad had dished up his news from Citizens' Bank at the dinner table while Mom and Grandmother served the fried chicken, mashed potatoes, gravy, and biscuits. By the time we took in Dad's news,

4

we stopped being hungry, and platters of my favorite food went cold.

If we were going to hold onto the farm, Dad, Mom, and I had to move to Cincinnati for ten months. That's how long it would take us to earn enough money to catch up with our back payments to Citizens' Bank.

Ten months in some noisy, dirty city — away from Grandmother and Gramps, Janis and my other friends, and Bessie, my favorite cow. How could this be happening to me?

2

We had just four weeks to get ready for our move to the city if I was to start school on time in September. Dad made the arrangements. His friend Vic Bono, who lived in Cincinnati, had offered him a job in his auto repair shop. (A long time ago Dad had taken a course with Vic, so he knew something about fixing cars.)

Vic also had a place for us to live — in an apartment over his father's grocery store. We wouldn't have to pay rent, but there was a hitch. Mom and I would have to work part-time in the store.

All of these plans made me feel how desperate our situation was, and there was nothing I could do about it.

The four weeks went by in a blur. We were so busy, I barely had time to feel sad.

Dad and Gramps harvested most of the sweet corn. We got the peppers and peaches frozen, the beans and tomatoes canned, and we made enough jams and jellies to open up a store of our own. Somehow I managed to finish carving the cedar frog to give to Janis as a going-away present.

We hadn't stopped working until that last night, when we loaded up the pickup for Cincinnati. Janis got to spend the night so she could see us off this morning.

Leaving Janis behind was bad enough, but it was awful to see Grandmother standing on the front porch, waving and trying hard not to cry. It made me want to start bawling. But I didn't because I figured Mom and Dad didn't need a crybaby on their hands.

I waved from the back of the pickup, where I was riding with baskets of bedding, pots, pans, and dishes. The only real furniture we were bringing to Cincinnati was the hand-carved wooden chest Gramps had made for me. I had helped whittle the handles, so I wasn't about to leave it behind. Besides, when Mom saw all the junk I was planning to take with me, she was glad it was getting hidden away in the chest.

We had been on the road since five o'clock that morning. Mom, Dad, and Gramps were up in front. Gramps was going to drop us off at Bono's grocery store. Then he would drive back to the

7

farm by himself. He needed the pickup on the farm, so we'd have to get around on foot or by bus in Cincinnati.

Mom suddenly knocked on the rear window to get my attention. She opened and closed her left hand once. That meant we'd be there in five minutes. Dad was now driving across the L & N Bridge over the Ohio River. We had left Kentucky and were riding into downtown Cincinnati.

When you're used to looking across acres and acres of swaying yellow wheat, a city skyline is a gray, stiff sight.

Suddenly Dad slowed down and parked. Then I saw it: Bono's Grocery Store. I don't know why, but in the middle of all this mess of concrete and brick, the store looked good to me. Maybe it was because of the fresh corn and peaches out front on the wooden stands. For a moment I almost felt like I was back where I started at five o'clock that morning.

No sooner had our truck stopped when this roly-poly man came running over to us with a big German shepherd at his heels.

"It's the Gormleys! They are here at last! Hey, Figaro, say hello to the Gormleys," he cried.

The man had curly gray hair and a big bushy mustache. It had to be Mr. Bono. The dog Figaro gave a sharp bark.

Mr. Bono opened the door of the pickup on the street side. Dad jumped down. And what did Mr. Bono do? He hugged and kissed Dad back and forth on both cheeks, just like in an Italian movie I saw one time. Then he ran around to the sidewalk, opened Gramps's door, and shook Gramps's hand up and down, up and down, like he was pumping water at the well. Then he got hold of Mom's arm, helped her down, and hugged and kissed her on both cheeks.

"Thank God, you've come! So good to see you, Gormleys!" Mr. Bono repeated.

What a character! Mom got all red, but she thought he was nice. I could tell.

"All morning long we waited and we waited for the Gormleys." He laughed the whole time he talked, and all the while Figaro sat next to him, his head cocked to one side, as if hanging onto every word.

"And look here!" Mr. Bono suddenly spotted me in the back of the pickup. "There is little Gormley!"

I knew I was going to get it, too. He laughed some more and waddled around to the back end of our truck and stood there, ready to help me jump off, even though I didn't need help. Then I got the bear-hug treatment. I felt embarrassed, but Mr. Bono was all right. That

I knew for sure, just by looking at him.

"When my boy Vic told me that you would come and stay here, it was like a gift from heaven." Mr. Bono kissed the fingers of one hand.

"Come," he said suddenly and lifted the box of dishes off the back of the truck. "You follow me. Figaro, you stay. Take care of the store."

Gramps and I just stood there and watched Mr. Bono. Dad scratched his head and laughed.

"Better follow the man's orders," he said.

But Mom was already at the back of the pickup pulling down the wicker basket of bedding.

"Come on, Kate," she called. "Grab hold of the other handle."

I grabbed my side of the basket and together we moved through a front door next to the store entrance. Twenty-one steps up a long, narrow stairway, and we were on an open second-floor landing. We practically bumped our wicker basket into Mr. Bono, who was standing at the top of the steps with his back to us. He stared at the room as if he were seeing it for the first time.

"This is it," Mr. Bono said in a hoarse whisper when we set the basket down. He looked at the room and then down at his feet. He had been so happy before. Suddenly, he looked sad. I took one look at the apartment and knew why.

What a pit! The room we were standing in was

big and bare, except for a bed stuck under two dirty windows that looked out on the back of the building. On the floor was an old round rug the color of a moldy pond. The only uglier thing in the room was the wallpaper, pink roses floating and peeling off the chicken-gravy background.

"Nobody has lived here for thirty years." Mr. Bono raised his head just high enough to look me in the eye. "So I bought some nice white paint to fix up the place. Then my wife gets sick again. And there's no time to fix up the place nice for the nice Gormleys."

He looked like he was about to cry.

"Don't worry, Mr. Bono." Mom was swallowing hard. "We'll make out just fine, I'm sure."

She looked back at Dad and Gramps, who had just come up the steps with my carved chest. They set it down in the middle of the room and just stared. Both of them looked as though they'd been swatted across their faces with one switch of Bessie's tail.

"It certainly has an interesting floor plan." Mom had recovered and was walking into the room next to the stairway. It turned out to be a bedroom over the street, and it was just as ugly as the living room.

"I'm sure the white paint you bought will help

11

some, Mr. Bono," Mom said. She moved on to the next doorway. We all followed her like a funeral procession into the darkest, dreariest kitchen I'd ever seen.

"The stove and the refrigerator, they are old," said Mr. Bono, as if he were begging Mom to love them like long lost relatives. "But they work real well, Mrs. Gormley. Real well."

"That's nice," Mom said politely. She opened the last door off the open room into a bathroom. I got a glimpse of yellow fish swimming on a dirty blue sea of wallpaper.

"Look, Kate," Mom said, "the tub is up on legs."

"Just like home," I answered, giving her a look out of the corner of my eye.

"Then you'll stay?" Mr. Bono's hands were together under his chin, like he was praying for some big miracle.

Dad and Gramps looked at Mom, and she looked at me.

"We'll stay," she said in that definite voice she used for special occasions when nothing was going to budge her.

Downstairs a phone rang in the store. A screen door slammed. A bell jingled. Figaro barked.

"My customers! I forgot about my customers!" Mr. Bono ran to the steps. "I'll be back. You stay. That is good. That is very good!"

Mr. Bono wiped his denim apron across his forehead. "Good! Good! Good!" He repeated over and over as he disappeared down the stairs.

"Not good!" Gramps said to the rest of us. "Not good at all."

"All we have to do is paint." I couldn't believe the words were coming out of my mouth.

"Kate's right," Mom said. "Mr. Bono has already bought the paint. All we have to do is dig in and do it."

"This place will look like home in no time." I pulled a loose pink paper rose off the wall, and I thought about what happened to people who lied.

Dad and Gramps stood in the middle of the room and stared at nothing in particular.

"It's going to be fine, men," Mom said finally. "Our stay in the city will be over before we know it."

That was going too far with the lying, so I kept my mouth shut.

"True," Dad said. "Ten months is not forever, I guess."

Ten months was probably longer than forever, I was thinking as I continued to pick at an ugly bouquet of wallpaper roses.

"Gramps," Mom hugged him fast, "why don't you go now before we all start crying?"

"Good idea," said Dad, putting his arm around Gramps's shoulders.

"Lie a little, Gramps," I said. "Tell Grandmother everything here is perfect."

"I never bother to lie," Gramps said. "I just won't mention anything at all."

"I'll walk you down to the pickup, Gramps."

"Good. I need somebody to see me off good and proper."

We got down to the street, and Gramps gave me his Grizzly-Bear-Hug-Special.

"Kate," he said, "I put something at the bottom of your wooden chest. It's a brown-paper package you can go ahead and open when you get especially homesick."

"Then I am going to go up right now and open it," I said.

"No, Kate. Not now. Better save it. You are going to need it a lot more later on." Gramps started up the truck. "Just remember," he called back, "the bottom of your chest." And he was gone.

I watched him go, and for once, I knew that Gramps was wrong. Things couldn't get any worse. I ran up the steps and headed straight for my wooden chest, which had been left sitting near the alcove window in the open room.

"Kate, what in the world are you up to?" Mom

was beating a dusty mattress with a broom while Dad held it out the window fire escape.

"I'm looking for something that Gramps left for me." I had the lid of my chest pulled up, and was ready to dig down to the bottom.

"Later, young lady." Mom set the mattress back on the bed by the window and started rolling up the moldy pond rug.

"Your mom needs you right now, Kitten," Dad said. "I have to go and see Vic about my work schedule." He looked relieved to have an excuse to get out of this dump.

"Ben, please take this awful rug with you." Mom was whipping around the room like a tornado. "I saw a dumpster in the alley right behind the store. Pitch it in there, why don't you?"

"What do you want me to do, Mom?" I was eyeing my wooden chest and wondering if I could do two things at one time.

"You're in charge of sweeping and scrubbing this dreadful living room. I will tackle the kitchen." Mom's mouth was in a tight straight line. "And I do mean tackle." I had no choice but to take the broom Mom stuck in my hand.

Two hours' worth of sweeping and scrubbing didn't make this dump look much better. I looked over at Mom and I could tell she was coming to the same conclusion.

15

"Kate, it looks like that little alcove off the living room is going to have to be your bedroom." She leaned on her mop and pushed a stray wisp of hair off her face. I could see her eyes filling up.

I was so tired of seeing people cry. I looked away from her, over at the windows in the alcove.

"It's OK, Mom. Look, there's a wooden rod across the top of the alcove. There must have been a curtain that hung here at one time to separate it from the living room. Maybe if we hang something over the rod, it will look more like a real-honest-to-goodness bedroom."

"You could be right." Mom ran her hand over her eyes.

I climbed out the window of the alcove onto the fire escape and grabbed hold of the tall, scrawny tree that was trying to reach up past the sooty old buildings.

"How lucky can I get?" I yelled to Mom as loud as I could. "I've got my own private balcony and three hundred roofs to check out every day for ten months."

She laughed a little. "Just what you've always dreamed of, I know. Come on in now, Kate. Back to work for both of us."

All the time we were working, we could hear the bell on Mr. Bono's screen door jingling and his phone and cash register ringing.

"Help! Can someone help me?" a faraway voice was calling. Was there a ghost here, too?

Mom and I stared at each other.

"What do you say, Little Gormley? Can you come quick?"

There it was again. Now we both knew it was no ghost. Just Mr. Bono.

3

"**K**ate, you'd better get down there. Mr. Bono sounds so excited. I can't tell whether he's being robbed or he needs his phone answered."

Mom took the scrub brush out of my hand. I raced down the steps and into the long, narrow store.

"Oh, thank you, Little Gormley! My fruit stand out front, can you watch it? Help the people out there so I can take care of things inside. OK? You'll do it?"

As he talked, Mr. Bono fitted his wife's apron around me. It went around five times, practically.

While I was being fitted, I had a chance to check out the store. There were shelves from the bare wooden floors all the way up to the ceiling. They were all filled nice and neat with cans and boxes. All across the back of the narrow store was a meat counter, and up front by the door and display window was one of those tall, ancient, fancy brass cash registers. Figaro lay by the front door, checking everyone who walked in.

"The people passing by out front, they always try to squeeze my peaches. You help the ones who need help, and you say no in a nice way to the ones who want to squash my produce. You do that. OK, Little Gormley?"

So I tried to do what Mr. Bono said. But people are people everywhere, I figured. After an hour of waiting on them, I knew they just couldn't help squeezing the peaches, poking the plums, and popping ripe cherries into their mouths. Just like they couldn't help all the laughing and talking back and forth.

"And you must be Kate Gormley."

It was a voice out of nowhere, soft and quivery, an old woman's voice. I was scooping up cherries by the handfuls and dropping them onto the scale, so my back was to her voice.

"Yes, ma'am. I am Kate Gormley." I turned around to face her. She was no taller than I was, but bent over and resting on her cane.

"Do I know you from somewhere, ma'am? You look familiar."

"I'm Eliza McCracken. At another time and in another place we could have known each other, Kate Gormley. Mr. Bono tells me you are from near Groverville, Kentucky. I know Groverville, because we came from Topperville a long, long time ago."

"That's about one hundred miles from where we live, ma'am," I said. "I never expected to find anybody from near home in this place."

"Oh, don't go fooling yourself, young lady. You're not alone here." Eliza McCracken had a laugh that rang like a soft bell. "You've got more company than you know about, right here within ten blocks. And they're all here for the same reason, I expect. . . . They all came looking for the money tree."

"Oh, we're not looking for any money tree here, ma'am. We're just going to stay for a bit so we can meet the loan on our farm."

"Well, now, Kate Gormley, that's what we all say. Just stay long enough so we can get enough money together to go back and live in the sweet country air." Mrs. McCracken patted my arm gently. She whispered so that nobody but me could hear her. "But a year becomes fifty years before you know it."

"No!" I shouted and backed away like she'd slapped me.

For a minute she looked like she was losing her balance on the cane. I reached out to hold onto both her arms.

"No," I said more quietly. "Ten months is all we need."

"With all my heart, I hope so, Kate Gormley." Mrs. McCracken patted my arm again and smiled.

"I'm glad Mr. Bono has help." She seemed to be changing the subject. "He needs you more than you know. Now I'm going to pick out two peaches and two apples, and don't you fret about me handling the fruit. I've been doing this so long that I can pick the best fruit just from sight."

"Yes, ma'am." I felt shaky all over.

"There now. How much do I owe you?"

"That'll be eighty-five cents, Mrs. McCracken."

"Just call me Eliza. We're going to be great friends, you and I. Tomorrow, when you deliver my grocery order, you stop in for a nice sit-down conversation. What do you say to that?"

"Yes, ma'am."

"Eliza. Call me Eliza."

"Yes, Eliza, ma'am." It was hard to unlearn what you've been taught forever.

"That's a little better, Kate." She laughed her soft bell laugh again and hobbled up the steep hill of Park Street.

I didn't have time to think about what Mrs. McCracken said, because Mr. Bono was knocking

21

on his store window from inside. He pointed out two more people waiting to be helped.

When it finally quieted down and I had a minute to myself, I figured I hadn't done too badly my first day on the job.

"Hey, girl. What do you think you're doing?" some boy shouted from across the street.

I didn't like the sound of his voice.

"She's working for Bono. That's what she's doing." The girl with him answered before I could open my mouth.

I didn't much care for her voice, either. I watched the two of them cross in the middle of the street and come toward me, holding up their hands and stopping traffic like they owned the whole street.

They were both pale and skinny with stringy blond hair. Brother and sister, I was guessing. The boy looked a little older than the girl. She was about my age. I thought they looked as mean as snakes, ready to strike.

I felt myself getting angry.

"My name is Kate — not 'girl,' " I said, looking them both in the eye. Then I jerked my finger toward the girl. "And she's right. I work for Mr. Bono."

"Don't be pointing your finger at my sister,

girl," the boy said. "We don't take nothing from nobody."

"Same here," I said, staring a hole right through his watery, blue eyes.

"You watch the way you talk, girl," the sister said. "I got the toughest brother on Park Street, and I'm talking Upper and Lower Park combined. And I'm going to let you in on a little secret. We don't like the idea that you are working for Bono. Get it?"

"That's your tough luck." I was tired of listening to them and their threats.

"Wrong, girl. It's your tough luck." The boy's voice went through my head like old Dr. Duffy's dentist drill. "I let Bono know a long time ago that I could use a job working here."

"And no new girl beats my brother out of a job, without hearing from us," said the sister.

"And who in his right mind is going to give your old brother a job?" I said through my teeth.

"Obviously not Bono." The girl laughed a great big hyena laugh.

"Shut up, Juanita. Me and girl here are going to talk some serious business. I'm telling you right now who's going to give me a job."

He took a step closer to me.

"You, girl. That's who. I'm going to protect you

while you deliver your groceries, and you'll pay me half of what you make from old Bonehead Bono."

"Hey, Freddy, cool it!" Juanita said, dipping into the seedless grapes and popping a handful into her mouth. "That's blackmail."

"And what you're doing is called stealing." I stared at her so hard, she looked away.

"You think about my offer, girl, and if I don't hear from you, you'll be hearing from me," said Freddy. He started walking up the street.

I cupped my hands and shouted back at him, "Don't hold your breath, buster!"

"Hey, Little Gormley! What's all this shouting about?" Mr. Bono was at his front door, wiping his hands on his apron. He looked up the street and saw the girl and boy strutting along.

"Don't let me ever catch you talking to those Wolcott kids again. They are the worst, those two!"

"You don't have to tell me," I said and I could feel my eyes tearing up. I was mad.

"It's hard being away from home, Little Gormley." He patted me on the shoulder. "Don't think I don't know how you feel. I was just like you when my family came to this country from Italy." Mr. Bono's eyes started filling up at the memory.

"But don't worry," he said. "The years pass, and things, they get better."

"No." It came out of my mouth in a choke. "We're not staying here for years. Ten months. That's it. Ten months!"

He didn't say anything. Silently we took in the baskets of produce. It was closing time.

4

I didn't know there was this much bad luck. I was having it all, sitting in a strange school with the only two people in the whole world I couldn't stand. The Wolcotts, Freddy and Juanita, were both in my fifth-grade class! Maybe they were twins. For me they were Double-Trouble all right.

"What'dya know?" said Freddy on the first day of school after Miss Applegate, the teacher, introduced me to the class. "Bono's little helper is a hayseed from the Kentucky sticks."

"Take a walk, Freddy," said Miss Applegate. "Get a drink of water while you're out in the hall, and come back with a new attitude."

Juanita started giggling like a hyena at her funny, funny brother. "And you'll control yourself, Juanita," the teacher said, "right now."

That seemed to take care of them for the time being, but it was an hour before I could even look up from my desk. It took me that long to decide there was nothing else to do but ignore the Double-Trouble Wolcotts for the next ten months. Ten months! The thought made me sick!

I looked up and saw Miss Applegate working with Freddy's reading group. She's the only good news around. She never seemed to let Freddy get to her. She said funny things, and I knew I was going to like her. Most of all, she's cool. She didn't even blow up at Freddy. I could hear him now, stumbling over some words in his book. Suddenly, he threw it down on the floor. "I'm not gonna read any more of this garbage," he said.

"Pick up the book, Freddy. Right now," Miss Applegate said. "There'll be no more pity-parties for you. If you knew all these words, you wouldn't need to be here, and I'd be out of a job. Let me read it to you. Now listen, because you're going to like this story."

She read while Freddy picked up his book. If I were Miss Applegate, I would have expelled him yesterday. But I wasn't. I was just Kate Gormley from near Groverville, Kentucky, wanting to be back there in my own schoolhouse.

A shrill bell rang and made me jump a foot.

"Let's line up for lunch." Miss Applegate bounded out of her chair. "I'm hungry."

She came over, put her arm around me, and signaled to another girl across the room.

"Laura, will you show Kate where the lunchroom is? I'll put both of you in charge of the dodgeball for after lunch." She led the class into the hall.

"Careful, Laura-girl," Freddy said under his breath. "Don't get too close to Hayseed Gormley. You might catch some of them country cooties she brought with her."

The kids in line laughed like they thought that's what they'd better do, or else. The girl called Laura turned red. "Here," she said, not looking me square in the eye, "you take the ball."

"Thanks a whole lot," I said and stared a hole through her dumb old forehead, so that she had to look at me.

I felt like a fool carrying the yellow ball through the hall and down to the lunchroom. When I picked up my lunch tray, I tried tucking the stupid thing under my arm while I balanced the trayful of food with the other. It was a disaster! I couldn't juggle the milk, the grilled cheese sandwich, and the bowl of vegetable soup, so I dropped the tray. The ball fell out from under my arm and knocked the soup bowl onto the floor and broke it. From there it rolled all over the lunchroom floor, making soup marks.

Everybody in the cafeteria looked up.

"Hay-Hay-Hayseed Gormley! That's her name! What's her game? Making messes! Making messes!" Freddy chanted. He beat a rhythm with his spoon on the soup bowl.

"Hey, Freddy, look at her." Juanita wanted to get into the act. "She doesn't even know enough to put the ball in the ball box before she gets in the lunch line. How stupid can you get?"

So that's what I was supposed to do with the ball! I glared at Laura. But she had her head bent down so close to her soup, she looked like she was finding all kinds of cartoons in the bowl.

Some teacher on duty picked up the ball and quieted down the Wolcotts, and the custodian came over with a mop to clean up my mess. So while everyone was busy, I put away my tray and made a break for the playground.

Once I got outside, I realized the playground was no better than the lunchroom. No tree to climb. No place to go and hide. No privacy. No nothing. I was glad when the bell finally rang so that we could line up and go in.

Math was in the afternoon. I wasn't crazy about math, but it sure was better than lunchtime. Then came social studies and, finally, a movie about keeping healthy. I figured I could make my own health movie: Get out of this city and go back to the farm. That'd be the best kind of health movie I could think of. Then, just before the dismissal bell, Miss Applegate gave us our homework assignments.

"How did your first day go, Kate?" Miss Applegate smiled at me and patted my shoulder as we lined up.

"It was different, ma'am." I couldn't believe I was being so polite about this rotten first day in this rotten place.

"Listen to her," Freddy snorted as we left school. "I'll bet it's different. I'll bet they don't even have school where you come from, Hayseed."

Suddenly I'd had enough of Freddy and Juanita Wolcott. "Then, Wolcott," I said, "how come I can read and multiply, and you can't?" It was out of my mouth before I could stop it. Now I'd do anything to take it back. But there it was, hanging heavy on the air between them and me.

I didn't like the look that came over Freddy's face. The other kids saw it, too, and took off in all directions.

"You'll be sorry for that crack, girl," Juanita said. For once I agreed with her.

5

I walked past the Wolcotts and went on to Bono's Grocery Store. Why couldn't I keep my mouth shut? But, then again, why should I, when those creeps were bullying me? So it was over, but not done with. Freddy would try to make me pay.

When I reached home, the first thing I wanted to do was run upstairs and throw myself across the bed by the alcove window. But Mr. Bono and Mom had other plans.

"Kate, you don't have time to change clothes." Mom was at the cash register, ringing up orders like she'd been doing it all her life.

"I need you, Little Gormley." Mr. Bono came out from behind the meat counter and put a package of meat in a grocery cart already loaded with bags of groceries.

"Our customers, Little Gormley!" He moved his hand across the tops of the bags in the cart. "They call in their orders all day long now that they know

31

I have a speedy delivery service. They wait for you so that they can start supper."

All the while Mr. Bono talked, Figaro stood next to the cart with his head cocked to one side, whining and crying.

"No, Figaro. No, boy." Mr. Bono shook his finger at the poor dog. "Little Gormley doesn't have time to be bothered with you."

Figaro stopped whining. He hung his head and went over by the counter under the cash register to lie down. He seemed so pathetic with his face between his two front paws that I felt drawn to him. He looked the way I felt, and he was doing just what I would have liked to do if only everybody would have left me alone.

"Here's a map, Little Gormley. I drew it all out for you," Mr. Bono said. "You've got ten deliveries. Now look here. I put Eliza McCracken last on your list. She lives right up over Stoob's Bakery. You know the bakery on the corner? That's Stoob's. When she called me today, she got all excited to learn that you're going to deliver her groceries. She says she's got lots to talk to you about." Mr. Bono laughed.

"Don't let her keep you all night with her talk. I want you back here before dark, so I don't worry, right?"

"Right, Kate," said Mom in that firm voice as she opened the door to let me out of the store.

Mr. Bono handed me the map he'd drawn. He lined up the names and addresses written on the bags with where they belonged on the map. Before I had any more time to think about my big problem, I was out of the store and back on Park Street, pushing a cartful of brown grocery bags.

Once I got the hang of it, things went pretty easily. Most of the apartments were right on the main street. Sometimes the people lived four and five flights up, and most of them were older and had trouble getting around. One lady was even in a wheelchair. Some grabbed their groceries, paid me, and locked up real fast. Others wanted to talk about troubles I'd never have thought of in a million years. I almost felt like forgetting my own problems.

In fact, I was even beginning to feel lucky. I had two more stops to make, and I hadn't thought of the Wolcotts once. Pretty soon I could go home and eat. I was starved.

I got to the top of the hill and left Eliza's bag of groceries in the cart next to Stoob's Bakery Shop. Then I ran up three flights with my biggest bag. When I came back down, all ready to deliver Eliza's bag next door, it was gone. A carton of eggs from the bag had been smashed against Stoob's Bakery window. Egg yolks were hardening as they dribbled down onto the sill.

A red-faced man wrapped up in a white gown and wearing a tall white baker's hat was standing in front of the window with his arms folded over his chest. I guessed it was Mr. Stoob, the baker. And was he ever mad!

"So! You are the one responsible!" he said, unfolding one arm and pointing at his messy window. "Clean it up, young woman. Do it right now, or I'll call the police."

"Those eggs came out of one of my grocery bags, so I'll clean it up. But I didn't do it," I answered.

"I never said you did!" He was so angry his voice was shaking. "But anyone dumb enough to leave anything unattended so those Wolcott brats can get at it is asking for trouble."

"The Wolcotts?" I yelled. "You mean you just stood there and watched them do it? You didn't even try to stop them?"

"Who says I didn't try to stop them? Why do you think this big egg mess is here? Juanita Wolcott heard me yelling at them to stop. She threw the eggs at my window, and they both took off."

"D.D.T. strikes again," I mumbled under my breath.

Mr. Stoob calmed down just enough to hear me. "What's that all about?" he said. "D.D.T.?"

"It stands for Double, Double Trouble." I began picking up the broken eggshells off the sidewalk, and I threw them in the torn bag that I'd found a few feet away.

"D.D.T." Mr. Stoob said it slowly like he was tasting the sound of it. "I like it. Best name I've ever heard for those two. D.D.T. Yes sir, that's a good one. You stay right here, young lady. I'll get us some buckets of water and some rags, and we'll both get this job done nice and fast."

In the fifteen minutes it took to clean up the big window, I introduced myself to Mr. Stoob and he gave me the word on the Wolcotts. Freddy and Juanita weren't twins, after all. Freddy had been held back twice, once in the first grade and once in the fourth.

"The father walked out on them when Juanita was still a baby," said Mr. Stoob, giving a stubborn egg lump a scrape with his nail. "And that was the good news, because Mr. and Mrs. Wolcott fought like cats and dogs when they were together. They made so much noise, no one in the neighborhood could sleep at night. If that Wolcott man hadn't left, there would have been murder and mayhem by and by."

"It looks like the father put Freddy and Juanita in charge of the mayhem part when he left." I gave my part of the clean window one final polish with the dry cloth.

"You're right, Kate." Mr. Stoob was scrubbing the sidewalk so hard with his push broom, I expected the concrete to start bleeding.

"You know, Kate, you're going to have to figure out a way to protect your bags while you're delivering groceries."

"I expect you're right, Mr. Stoob. They sure do have it in for me."

"Don't think for a minute that you're alone, Kate. Freddy Wolcott has it in for every storekeeper up and down Park Street."

"You want to know why he has it in for me, Mr. Stoob?" I said. "He thought he ought to have the job I've got delivering groceries for Mr. Bono."

"Ha! That's a good one!" said Mr. Stoob. "Who in his right mind would hire Freddy Wolcott to do anything? I could use a little help around here myself, but I'll tell you one thing . . . it wouldn't be one of the Wolcotts."

I stepped back to survey the whole window. "I think it's all clean now, Mr. Stoob."

"I like your spirit, Kate Gormley." Mr. Stoob had put aside his broom and was shaking my hand. "Whenever you have groceries to deliver up this way, you just park your cart inside my shop. I'll watch it for you."

"Thanks, Mr. Stoob. I've got to go back and refill Eliza McCracken's order and get it to her before it gets too dark."

"I'll be here for a while," said Mr. Stoob. "I'll be on the lookout for you."

By the time I'd walked back to the store, Mr. Bono and Mom were getting ready to close up.

"Little Gormley, where have you been? I got worried when you didn't come back."

"Eliza McCracken's groceries got totaled, Mr. Bono. Can I refill the order real fast?"

"Kate, how in the world did that happen?" Mom was giving me the look she saved for special occasions.

"The cart overturned, Mom."

It wasn't the whole truth, but it was good enough for an emergency. If Mom and Mr. Bono knew that the Wolcotts had done it, they probably wouldn't let me go out alone. And that would be the end of my salary, which was going to help us get out of this totally rotten place.

"Don't be mad, Mrs. Gormley. I'll refill the order right now, Little Gormley. I don't want trouble between you."

"No, Mr. Bono. You're all set to go home." Mom's voice matched her look. "I'll refill the order, and Kate will reimburse you for your losses."

Before Mr. Bono and I knew what was happening, we were both on our way. He went to his house, and I went back to Eliza's.

Mr. Stoob meant what he said. He was there at his window waving at me when I ran up the steps to Eliza's apartment above.

"Kate Gormley, there you are!" Eliza held open her front door and signaled me through the living room with her hand. "I've been waiting and waiting to have a nice little sit-down chat with you all about down home."

It was a funny thing. When Eliza said the words *down home*, I knew what she meant. Even though I was moving quickly through the living room and the dining room and into the kitchen, heavy load and all, I could tell this was home. Everything about it was home. There were lace doilies with embroidered pillows on the armchairs, samplers and family pictures on the walls, and jars of preserves lined up on the kitchen cabinet.

"Hand me those cans, will you, Kate?" Eliza asked. "I declare they get heavier and heavier for me to lift out of the grocery bag. Good. Now, just put that milk in the refrigerator, and I'll fix us a nice cup of tea, and we'll have some homemade cookies and a good talk."

"Oh, Eliza, I can't stop today. It's real late, and I am in big trouble with my mom."

"Well, now, we can't have your mama angry with you, that's the truth." Eliza sounded disappointed. I could tell by the way she was looking at the plate of cookies.

"Next time I'll be able to visit longer," I told her, "because I'll know my way around here better."

"Here, Kate. I'll bag up these cookies for you and your family. It's an old recipe that's been in my family for four generations. Maybe biting into some of that old Kentucky sweetness will keep your mama from being too mad at you." Eliza handed me the bag of cookies, put her arm around my shoulder, and led me to the door.

"Eliza, why did you ever leave home in the first place?" I blurted it out, because I just couldn't help it, I guess. I had to know.

Eliza did not seem surprised. She put her hand on the front doorknob and stood there a long time without saying anything. When she did speak, her voice seemed sad and tired.

"We were young then, Kate. Charlie and I were just fresh married and full of dreams. The men in both our families had been coal miners for generations. They had died young, all of them. Black lung disease got them in the end. We didn't want that to happen to us and to our children. So we decided to come to the city and shake the money tree."

"What did you want all that money for, Eliza?"

"Now, why do you ask that, Kate Gormley?" Eliza McCracken laughed a sad, soft laugh. "We were going to save every single penny and then we were going to run back home as fast as we could and buy us a farm."

"And what happened?"

"I bet you already know the answer, since you're looking me square in the eye. First baby comes along. Then the second one comes. And the third. You start getting to know the doctor pretty well. Then you have to buy a bad secondhand car. Then that car needs big repairs. Before you know it, you're glued to the city like pitch to the road."

Eliza shook her head as if she were waking from some kind of trance. She turned the doorknob and opened the door.

"Now get along with you, Kate Gormley. I don't want your mother to be mad at me, too. We'll have us a nice visit, you and me, one of these days. Safe home, now."

6

"What took you so long, Kate?" Mr. Stoob was locking the door to his bakery shop. "I almost went up there to get you."

It was the third time somebody had told me I was taking too long. "I guess I got carried away with talk, Mr. Stoob," I said, taking a deep breath. "Thanks for waiting."

"You're all right, Kate Gormley. You take care now, and you be sure to have a good evening."

I nodded but kept my thoughts to myself. I was definitely not going to have a good evening. That much I knew.

When I got home, I kept waiting for Mom to light into me. But all through dinner she was quiet. Then, whammo! Right when I got into my pajamas and crawled in under the covers, she came over and sat on the edge of my bed.

"Kate, that refill order is going to cost five dollars and seventy-five cents. That's bad enough, but if it happens again, I think Mr. Bono will find someone who is more responsible to do the job. Isn't what we're doing here important to you at all?"

"Thanks a lot, Mom!" I could feel my mouth taking over my body. I started to say more, but Mom put her finger to my mouth.

"Watch your tongue, Katherine Ann Gormley!"

That did it. First the Wolcotts. Then the whole dumb school, plus this stupid city. And now my own mother. I pushed her hand away from my mouth, closed my eyes, and turned in my bed away from her. I heard her sigh and walk across the open room to their bedroom. I could hear her talking in a soft voice to Dad. About me? Was she going to turn him against me, too? Why not turn everybody against dumb old Katherine Ann Gormley?

The lights in their bedroom went off. It was dark, except for the red and blue lights that were flashing on and off on the cigarette signboard two blocks over. Mom and Dad were asleep.

I sat up crosslegged on my bed, looking out of the alcove windows. What a nasty view! A poor old scrawny tree spotlighted in the red and blue fluorescent lights, rubbing its ugly old branches against a rusty fire escape. And if I got tired of that view, I could always watch rooftops and chimneys jagging against the black sky in the city of Cincinnati.

Suddenly, I knew this was the day Gramps had meant. The day when I couldn't get more homesick.

I opened the lid of my wooden chest and did some digging. I found the package at the bottom and tore it open. And there it was, Gramps's pocketknife. There were also two chunks of basswood from the tree we cut down last spring.

Nothing meant more to Gramps than his whittling knife with the ivory handle. It had been his father's, my great-grandfather's. Gramps had told me once that it was eighty years old. He used to joke that it meant so much to him he wanted to take it with him in the next life. And now, here it was . . . with me.

"Gramps, what's gotten into you?" I said in a whisper. "Your whittling knife, of all things." And then I saw his note. I opened it and read:

Dear Kate,
   I reckon you're mighty low right now. Otherwise, you wouldn't be reading this. You're sick for home, and you don't think you can be happy any other place.

43

*But you are wrong, Kate. You don't
find happiness. You create it. And you
can make happiness anywhere you go
with your own hands and heart, Kate,
because you are a whittler.*

*That means you have the magic
touch. It's up to you to shape a part of
your world just the way you want it.
So take my knife, Kate, and whittle
away. Give that new place your magic
touch.*

All my love and my faith in you,
Gramps

I didn't know I was crying until I saw drops
spilling down on the paper.

"Oh, Gramps!" I cried into the pillow. "I can't
make anything out of this pit of a place. I hate it.
I'll always hate it. And you're wrong. I can't ever
be happy here. I can only be happy at home, where
I belong."

I lay there, face down, until I couldn't stand
the wetness of the feather pillow anymore. I
turned over and felt around the bed for Gramps's
knife and the damp note. In the darkness I
wrapped the note around the ivory-handled knife.

I held on tight, waiting for some magic to pass from the knife to me. I tossed and turned in bed. One after another, the two basswood chunks fell off the bed and onto the bare wooden floor.

7

The next morning I was awake before Mom. That hardly ever happened. When I opened my eyes, I could feel the stillness of the apartment. I closed them again and tried to remember what had happened last night. Then it all rushed back. Gramps and his ivory-handled pocketknife. And his note. I was still holding onto both in the fist of my hand. I didn't even have to read the note to remember his words.

You don't find happiness, you create it. So take my knife, Kate, and whittle away. Give that new place your magic touch.

"You wouldn't say that, Gramps, if you knew what I know about this place."

I was wide awake now, talking to him a mile a minute. While I talked, I looked out the window at that poor excuse of a tree with one of its dead twigs scratching across the windowpane.

"Look at it, Gramps. Just take a look. Maybe

it wouldn't be so bad if I could have a decent tree with some hummingbirds whizzing all around. But, no. Look what I'm stuck with every morning of my life for the next ten months. A dumb old scraggly tree that no respectable bird would come near. Not even a Cincinnati bird, I'll bet."

I stopped. I wished Gramps would give me some answers, but I knew he couldn't, because he was two hundred and twenty miles away. I closed my eyes, and suddenly I remembered one day last spring walking under our red buckeye tree with Gramps. It was our favorite tree, Gramps's and mine. We had stopped and looked up. It was in full bloom and teeming with hummingbirds winging away at the red buckeye blossoms.

I looked down at the quilt Grandmother had made for me. Tree-of-life pattern, she called it. Nice bright trees made from bits and pieces of my outgrown clothes. Each tree had been sewn on a square of white cotton. My hand moved from one tree to another, and a feeling for the farm came over me so strong I had to shut my eyes.

That was when this crazy picture flashed inside of my head. I opened my eyes and looked up at the wooden rod that connected one side of the alcove to the other. I could hang my quilt on it and make this alcove into a real bedroom!

I pulled the ladder out of the closet and set it

up under the wooden rod. Then I took my quilt off the bed, climbed up to the wooden rod, and swung the quilt over the rod until it almost touched the floor. I pinned up the quilt so that the trees faced my bed and the plain white side faced the living room.

I climbed down the ladder and stepped back into the living room, so I could see how it looked. The white stitched back of the quilt looked like a fancy fourth wall of the living room.

I pulled aside my quilt wall and went into my bedroom. I sat on my bed and closed my eyes for a minute so that I could pretend I was seeing it for the first time. Then I opened them and looked. "Sixteen trees!" I counted them off, one by one. "My own handmade forest."

This was really going to work. I felt around the floor for the two chunks of basswood. Then I jumped up on my bed and held them near the rod. I'd whittle them into hummingbirds. I'd put them up so they'd be perched on either side of the rod. They would look like they were buzzing around my forest of trees.

"Kate, what in the world are you up to?" Mom's voice sounded muffled on the other side of my forest wall. Then there was a pause. "Well, would you look at this!" I heard her laughing softly on the other side of the quilt. "Shall I knock on your wall before entering?" She pushed the quilt over to one side and looked in. Then she came and sat down on the edge of the bed with me. We didn't say anything. We just sat there looking at the trees on my quilt.

"This must be the only bedroom in the world that looks like a Kentucky woods," Mom said softly. "I love it, Kate."

"Just wait," I said. "You're going to love it all the more when you see the hummingbirds I'm going to carve for the rod."

When Mom saw Gramps's whittling knife and the two chunks of basswood, she smiled and shook her head. "Well, now, isn't that something? And aren't you something, too, Kate." She gave me a quick hug. "I'm sorry about the things I said last night. I didn't mean them. I was just tired, I guess."

"I'm sorry about what I said. I was tired, too, Mom. Sick and tired of this dumb old place and some of the people in it, if you really want to know."

"Do you think we'll make it, Kate, you and I?" Mom tightened her hold on me like she was hanging on for dear life.

"You know we will." I felt myself sitting up straighter on the side of the bed. "I've got some things figured out today that I didn't have a clue about yesterday. So I guess that's something."

I got dressed and had some breakfast, with plenty of time left over before I had to leave for school. Enough time to get me started thinking about what Gramps had written about creating my own happiness. I dug down into my chest, dragged up my lunch box from Groverville School, and packed myself a lunch so I wouldn't have to hang out in that long lunch line. And when I finished packing my sandwiches, cookies, and apple, I slipped in the two chunks of basswood. I stuck Gramps's knife into the back pocket of my jeans and checked the clock.

It was time to go to school, and I was ready! As I went down the stairs, I could see Mr. Bono opening up the store. Figaro was right behind him.

"Be a good girl today, Little Gormley, so you don't have to stay after school." Mr. Bono's eyes were twinkling. "I've got lots of orders today, so I'll need you right after school, OK?"

It was strange how Gramps's message stayed with me, and everything started clicking in my head. I was standing there thinking about delivering all those groceries with the Wolcotts hot on my heels. It didn't seem like a big problem anymore.

"Mr. Bono, maybe I could take Figaro with me when I am delivering groceries?" I asked.

"You mean it?" Mr. Bono's eyes got big when I nodded yes. "Little Gormley, you've got lots of smarts. You know old Figaro needs some exercise. You know I can't get around like I used to. So you come up with this great idea. If you do that for Fig, I'll give you a dollar raise a week, right off the bat."

I kept hoping my luck would hold out. But when I got to school, I knew that there's only so much luck in the world. The school was just the way I left it — big, old, and gray. And the Wolcotts were just as mean and loud as ever.

I got through the morning without even looking at them or that Laura or any of those strangers because I was too busy thinking about something nice, like how I was going to work out my hummingbird shapes. I even finished my work early so that I could have some time to work out a sketch on paper. When I did look up, everyone was lining up for lunch.

I hung back and waited until there was enough confusion in the hallway to slip through the exit door to the playground. No more cafeteria for me!

"Katherine Ann Gormley," I said to myself, "somewhere out on that playground, you're going to find a private place away from all those rotten people."

From where I was standing, it didn't look too promising. I could see nothing but black tar that ended in a big cyclone fence six feet high. So I kept walking until I reached the far side of the school. And then I saw a tiny green patch of grass with a big oak tree shooting straight up to the sky like a giant green firecracker. Off to one side was a little swing set and a seesaw.

"For the nursery-school kids," I mumbled, "but who cares? I'm not particular." To me, it was like a beautiful, deserted island. I walked over to take a closer look at the rough, knobby roots of the old tree. The roots were so old they wouldn't give in to the tar, so the tar just quit and went around them. The trunk of the tree was as broad as I was with both my arms stretched out.

"It's a perfect match!" I said. I sat down under the tree. "And nobody in the world is going to know where I go at lunchtime."

I could hear the kids who had finished their lunch yelling and screaming on the playground, so I knew I'd be able to hear the bell when it rang. I opened my lunch box and pulled out my sandwich. I ate with one hand while I held a chunk of the basswood in the other, feeling the rough shape of it.

Gramps always said that wood will tell you something if you stay quiet and let it. I finished up the last bit of my peanut-butter-and-jelly sandwich and moved the chunk of basswood from one hand to the other, weighing it, rubbing it, studying it.

"Gramps is right," I said to the wood because I could see where the head of the hummingbird should be. And dead smack in the middle of where the head was supposed to be, I could see the eyes.

I pulled Gramps's knife from my pocket and speared the wood at the eyepoint. The tip of the knife juggled back and forth, nice and steady. I moved the knife to the other side of the head and made the second eye incision. And suddenly, I felt like I was home again, under a shady tree with a breeze blowing. Far away, I heard a bell ring. Fifteen seconds later, I realized what that bell meant.

I was out of breath by the time I caught up with the tail end of my class. I didn't look right or left, for fear someone would ask me where I had been.

When I got to my desk, I saw a folded up piece of paper on my chair. While Miss Applegate was getting the Wolcotts settled down, I opened it.

Be careful! W & W were looking for
you at lunchtime. Where were you?

Who cared enough to be warning me about the
W & Ws? I looked around the classroom. Some of
the kids didn't look too inhuman. No one was looking my way, though.

The afternoon clipped along pretty fast, and
then about twenty minutes before dismissal, Mr.
Ferguson, the principal, walked in and talked to
Miss Applegate. Dignified is the best way to de-
scribe Mr. Ferguson.

"Everyone, clear your desks and listen closely,"
Miss Applegate said. "Mr. Ferguson has some
good news for you."

"Boys and girls, Park Lane Public is going to
have its annual School Fair the week before
Thanksgiving," he said. "We'll have carnival
rides, refreshment stands, games, and prizes. But
the best part will be the classroom booths. I want
you to be thinking hard about the kind of booth
your class will develop this year."

A boy named Carl, who sat next to me, raised
his hand.

"Is the mayor going to be judging the booths
again this year?"

"Yes, he is, Carl," Mr. Ferguson said. "He and
two members of the Park Street Merchants' As-

sociation will decide which booth they think is the best. So begin planning today, and may the best booth win."

When Mr. Ferguson left, Freddy Wolcott turned to Miss Applegate and said, "I'm telling you right now, I've never been in a class that won."

"That's because you're a hex, Freddy." Juanita did her hyena giggle special.

I expected Freddy to laugh along with his sister, but instead, he glared at her.

"No, Juanita," said Miss Applegate. "You're totally wrong. Freddy is going to prove to you that this class, of which he's a part, is going to win."

I looked over at Freddy, and I couldn't believe what I saw. Old Paleface Wolcott Boy was blushing bright red. He acted as if no one in his life had ever had anything nice to say about him.

8

When the bell rang, Freddy became the Freddy we all knew and hated. He jumped out of his seat, jabbed the boy in front of him, and beat everyone, including Juanita, to the door.

"Freddy, would you mind staying after school for about ten minutes?" Miss Applegate asked. "I need some help with the chalkboards. Thank you very much."

Freddy didn't look like he wanted to stay, but he went back to his desk and slumped down in his seat.

"No, Juanita," said Miss Applegate to Girl Wolcott who sat down, too, as if she were her brother's Siamese twin. "You don't have to wait for Freddy. I'll drive him home a little later on."

Juanita followed me out of school and walked alongside me. She was lonesome without her brother, I guess. All I knew was that my luck had run out.

"Listen, girl, don't think for a second we've forgotten about you. You took away Freddy's chance for that job with Bonehead Bono. And you've got a real big mouth. We're going to get you good."

I kept walking and, most important of all, I kept my mouth shut.

"Where did you go at lunchtime, anyhow, Hayseed? You'd better not leave the playground at noon. That's breaking the big number-one school rule."

I couldn't keep quiet any longer. "And the only ones allowed to break school rules are the Wolcotts. Is that what you're trying to tell me?"

"You've got a lot to say for yourself, girl." Juanita didn't like anybody else to have the last word. Her face turned pink, and she stuck out her tongue at me.

"We'll see you this afternoon, when you're delivering Bonehead's groceries. You might be lonesome without us."

I started praying that old Figaro would be in the mood for a walk and maybe even a fight.

"Hey, Little Gormley, look at Figaro. He can't wait. Look at that tail go!" Mr. Bono said when I got to the store.

It was true. Figaro's tail was moving a mile a minute while he sat next to the cartful of groceries. I grabbed his leash and Mr. Bono's hand-drawn map, and we took off.

"Look out for the Wolcotts, Figaro." I whispered. "They're out to get me. And you've got to help me. D.D.T. or W & Ws, call them whatever you want to, Fig. They're bad news any way you look at them."

At first, nothing happened. I got through all of my stops except the last, without any more trouble from the Wolcotts.

My last delivery was two doors up from Mr. Stoob's Bakery. I tied Fig's leash to the cart. As usual, he sat quietly because he was so well trained. But when I got to the fourth-floor apartment, I heard Fig barking and growling so loudly I almost dropped my load. The lady answered the door, and I quickly exchanged the groceries for her money. Then I raced down the steps.

By the time I hit the first floor, I heard Freddy Wolcott yelling out things that he never learned in school. When I got to the sidewalk, Figaro had the D.D.T. Wolcotts nailed up against Stoob's Bakery window.

"Sit, Figaro. Sit, boy." I walked over and held Fig by the collar and petted him behind his right ear. "They won't hurt us, Figaro," I said in a sweet as sugar voice. "Just look at those cool Wolcotts crawling away. See how great Freddy and

Juanita can act when they don't have a choice."

Freddy and Juanita slinked along the window and then broke into a run. "Good boy, Figaro. Good boy." I could hardly stop laughing while I rubbed my face into his neck.

"You're a mighty clever girl, miss." Mr. Stoob was standing in the middle of his doorway with his tall white baker's hat off to one side.

"I started to come out. Then I saw that you and Figaro had everything under control." He laughed. "You beat those Wolcotts singlehandedly. Nobody has ever done that before. Do you know that? Wait right here. I've got something for you." He ran into the bakery and came out a second later with three of his super-big oatmeal cookies.

"You and Figaro need a little quick energy for all of your trouble, and I need one for all the energy I used up just watching you." Mr. Stoob started to laugh again.

"Thanks, Mr. Stoob."

Even though I was tired, I felt good walking home, chewing on my cookie. The Wolcotts had looked so funny pushed up against that window, scared out of their wits.

"Figaro! Figaro! Look at you!" Mr. Bono took the leash from me and started rubbing Fig's head. "You had a good day, eh, Figaro?"

59

"It looks like it was a good day all around. Right, Kate?" Mom glanced at me while she closed down the cash register.

"Right, Mom. Everything worked out even better than I figured it."

When Mr. Bono and Figaro left, I told Mom all about the mean Wolcotts.

"But, Kate, why didn't you tell me that yesterday? I feel even worse about snapping at you the way I did," Mom said.

"Forget about it, Mom. The thing to remember is seeing those Wolcotts backed up against Stoob's window, so scared that their hair was practically standing on end. That's the part to think about." I was laughing fit to kill.

But when I looked over at Mom, waiting for her to chime in, I could tell she didn't think it was funny.

"Maybe the Wolcotts are sort of like you and me, Kate," she said in a real quiet voice.

"The Wolcotts? Like us? Are you kidding? The Wolcotts are like nobody you'd ever want to know! I can't believe you said that, Mom."

"It sounds to me as if the Wolcotts feel like outsiders, Kate."

"Well, if they feel that way, they've sure got that right. Everyone who knows them, hates them."

Mom started upstairs to our apartment, then she stopped and waited for me to catch up. "So they must feel very left out in this city, right?"

"I guess so."

"That's all I'm saying, Kate. The Wolcotts are a little like us. They feel left out, the way we do right now."

The Wolcotts and us . . . alike? Oh, brother! I caught up with Mom on the stairs, and she put her arm around me. And for once I kept my big mouth shut.

9

I couldn't figure it out. Either I was getting tougher living in the city, or else the Wolcotts were getting quieter. They hadn't bugged me for four weeks, and I didn't mean four weeks of just school. I was talking about four whole weeks of total peace and quiet after school when Fig and I delivered groceries.

Good old Fig! I had a lot to thank him for. Not only did he get the Wolcotts off my back, he'd even gotten me a raise in salary — one extra dollar every week for taking Figaro with me for his daily walk. At first, I felt guilty about taking it, because, after all, Fig was helping me out. But Mr. Bono insisted. He said it was worth it to know that Figaro was getting proper exercise. So my bank account was getting fat. No one was bugging me, and I couldn't really complain.

Something else had happened. That girl, Laura,

who had sabotaged me on my first day of school, turned out to be OK. Don't go judging people until you've been around them for a while — that's what Gramps always says. And he was right in Laura's case. We became good friends, believe it or not.

It all happened a week or so after I found my lunchtime hideout. I was sitting under my tree, munching the sandwich I'd brought for lunch and whittling away at my hummingbird. The sun was shining through the tree, and I was feeling very peaceful. All of a sudden, this shadow fell across my lap, coming between me and the sun.

"So this is where you come every day at lunchtime. I've been looking all over for you," said a familiar voice.

I jumped about a foot high and looked up. It was Laura. "So what do you care where I've been?" I couldn't help the tone I was using on her.

"I guess you're still mad about that first day of school, aren't you?" She sat down on the grass across from me like she belonged there.

"Who, me? Mad at somebody who leaves me high and dry on my first day in a new school, and in a new city?" I didn't even bother to look at her. I was really wound up by then and couldn't stop myself. "Who, me? Mad at somebody who sticks me with a stupid ball that knocks everything off my dumb lunch tray? Whatever makes you think I'm mad?"

"Well, you don't have to get so sarcastic." Laura started sucking on a blade of grass as if she were really hurt. "I'm sorry about that day. But I was afraid that the Wolcotts would start in on me if I was nice to you."

"Thanks for nothing," I said. "We have a name for cowards back where I come from."

"Why don't you shut up and listen?" Laura yanked the blade of grass out of her mouth and glared at me. "I've been around the Wolcotts since I was in kindergarten. And if a Wolcott decides not to like you, your life isn't worth spit, if you'll pardon the expression."

"Yellow dog. That's what we call cowards down home, Laura."

"Call me whatever you want, Kate. All I know is that I've been able to steer clear of the Wolcotts all my life. I feel bad about that first day of school. And now, I also feel bad because the Wolcotts have been looking for you every day since you started disappearing at lunchtime."

"So, what's it to you? Look," I continued, "why don't you leave me alone." I said it calmly enough, considering the way she was butting into my private place. "I'm getting along just fine without having to deal with a yellow dog."

"That does it!" Laura jumped up. "I was trying to warn you about the Wolcotts because I felt bad about the way I ditched you on the first day of school." Laura talked slowly, as if I were some kind of dummy who wasn't getting her message. "I've been trying to make up for it, but never mind. I know when I'm not welcome." She turned and started to go.

"Are you the one who wrote the note about W & W?" I had to know.

Laura nodded her head yes.

"That's a good name for them. I call them D.D.T. Stands for Double, Double Trouble."

Laura laughed and bent over to pull up her sock. "You sure called that one right." Far away the bell was ringing.

"Do you think I could come back tomorrow and watch what you're doing?" Laura sure wasn't shy.

"I guess so, but don't be bringing W & W hot on your heels," I answered.

"Don't worry about me," Laura said. "I'm better at steering clear of D.D.T. than you are."

And before I could come up with an answer to that one, she was gone.

So Laura started coming every day that week.

By the end of the week, I had finished the first hummingbird, and Laura was sanding it for me. So I started carving the second one.

"I never saw a hummingbird before, but this sure is a pretty carving." Laura was wrapping the little piece of sandpaper around her thumb the way I'd shown her.

"Well, take my word for it. That's a life-size model of the real thing. It's exactly how they look when they're perched still for half a second. Usually they're flitting around, and their wings go so fast, you can't even see them."

"Tell me again about this wall you've made for your bedroom out of a quilt full of trees. I still don't understand how that works."

"Laura, I've drawn it for you. I've told you all I can. I don't know what else I can do to get it across to you," I answered.

"I should probably come by and see it," she said. "How about tonight after school?"

"Nothing like inviting yourself over."

"Kate, when you saw I didn't understand, you should've thought of inviting me over, before I had to force you into it," Laura replied.

One thing about Laura, she always tells you what's on her mind. So she came over that day after school, and really went crazy over my bedroom wall full of trees.

"Oh," she said, "that quilt is a wall. It's like a forest with all those bright trees. Why didn't you say so, Kate?"

"I *did!*"

But she paid no attention.

"And the two hummingbirds are going to perch on either side of the rod, like they're resting in the forest," Laura said.

"Just the way I drew it, Laura," I answered.

"And look! You really have made a room where there wasn't one before! And do you know why I love it so much?" Laura asked.

I didn't answer because I was too busy watching the look on her face. And besides, I knew she was going to keep on talking no matter what I did.

"Our apartment is just like yours. The only difference is that we're on the fourth floor. And guess who's stuck in the dumb little nothing area by the window? Just guess."

"You, Laura? Really?"

"Right! Me. And now I know just what I can do about it. My mom has an old bedspread I can nail across our archway. And when you get your other hummingbird whittled, you can do two for me, and I'll be all set. Just like you." She smiled at me.

"That's great," I said sarcastically. "You're giving me permission to carve two more humming-birds, just like that."

"No, not hummingbirds." Laura was too excited to catch my sarcasm. "I wouldn't know a hum-mingbird if it came and shook hands with me. I want something I can recognize, like sparrows. And don't be giving me that look, like I'm trying to put something over on you. I'll sand your hum-mingbirds and help you deliver groceries if you do my sparrows. OK?"

"OK. It's a deal. Sparrows are easy. But where are we going to get the wood?"

"No problem," said Laura. "There's a big dead tree that the city just cut down in the park on the next street over from me. There's plenty of good wood there. Let's go get it now," Laura said.

"Hey, not so fast, Laura. I've got my deliveries to do yet. By the time I get finished, it'll be dark."

"Kate, by the time you get finished, it will still be light, because I'm going to start helping you today. That was the deal, remember? Come on. Let's go."

We took off with Figaro and finished while it was still light. True to Laura's word, there was plenty of good wood stacked in logs off to one side of the park. The wood was pine, which is good for a beginner because it's so soft and easy to carve.

"Sometimes the city will cut the wood in log

sizes so that people who have woodstoves and fireplaces can use them," said Laura.

"Here are two pieces that won't go into fireplaces." I bent over and found two sparrow-sized chunks of wood, side by side.

"Good! Kate, why don't you finish up your hummingbird tonight, and I'll finish sanding the first one. Then tomorrow you can get started on my sparrow."

I laughed. "Laura, I wish you weren't so shy. I mean I really think you hang back too much."

"You ought to be glad I say what I think. We need more honest people like me in the world." Laura put her arm around my shoulder. "Now promise me you'll finish that hummingbird tonight."

"OK." I had to laugh, too. "I promise."

10

I did finish it. It took me about three hours. And the next day Laura beat me to our tree at lunchtime.

"Did you finish the second hummingbird? Good. I'll start sanding it. I'm finished with the first one, don't you think? How does it look?"

Laura was so excited that I didn't know what to answer first.

"The first one looks good, Laura. Yes, start on the second one. Yes, I think you're a good sander," I said.

"I think so, too." Laura sounded as if she were someone else. "It takes patience, persistence, and pushiness, and I've got plenty of all three. At least, that's what my mother tells me. I've been on her to get that old bedspread out of the trunk in the basement. Finally she gave in and went down, and guess what? She found two bedspreads. She came upstairs loaded down with them and all tired and crabby. And that's when she let me know about my patience, persistence, and pushiness."

"How does your room look?"

"Great! Mom wouldn't let me nail up the bedspread. She made my brother put up a curtain rod like yours. So I've got one bedspread on the curtain rod for my bedroom wall, and I'm using the other one on my bed. And when you finish my sparrows, we can give a grand tour of our two bedrooms, which we created out of nothing."

"I can see it all now. Our whole class coming and standing in line to get a look." I was getting into the right spirit. Laura did that to me.

"If the Wolcotts show up," Laura said, "we'll have to call the fire department and the police department, too."

"Laura, the Wolcotts are bad" — I couldn't keep from laughing — "but they can't be all that bad."

"Says who?" Laura stared me down. "When I was in kindergarten and Freddy was in first grade the second time, the fire department had to come and get him down from the ceiling in the boys' bathroom."

"How did that happen?"

"He had climbed up the wall and lifted out two ceiling tiles. He thought there was a secret passageway up there, and he got stuck in the pipes and couldn't get down."

"You've got to admit that's a pretty smart thing for a kid that little to think about," I said.

"They should have left him up there for good," Laura said. "And Juanita isn't much better than Freddy. In the second grade, our teacher decided to give little Juanita some class responsibilities. So she let her water the plants."

"That's not a bad idea."

"Not a bad idea for anybody but a Wolcott. The plants were all on the windowsill. The first day on the job, Juanita went over to the window and waited for somebody to walk by. Then she took the full pitcher of water and dumped it outside!" Laura exclaimed.

"What happened?" I asked.

"Guess who was the somebody walking by?"

"I give up. Who?" Laura got too dramatic when she told a story.

"Miss Wallendorf."

"You mean our assistant principal?"

"In person! So that was the end of Juanita's plant-watering days. After that, our second-grade teacher didn't take her eyes off Juanita for the rest of the year."

"Miss Applegate is real cool about having two Wolcotts in the class," I said.

"You bet she's cool. She never even sends them down to the office," Laura said. She was sanding very hard, almost as if she wanted to smooth off the rough edges of the Wolcotts. "But, Kate, I only hope she doesn't let the Wolcotts ruin our booth at the School Fair."

I remembered Mr. Ferguson making his announcement about the School Fair and Freddy saying he would never be in a class that won a prize.

"We're guaranteed losers with those two in our class," Laura said, as if she were reading my mind.

"Wait, Laura! I just thought of an idea for a booth."

"What?" Laura put down her sandpaper. "Tell me, quick."

"Why don't we have a sideshow at the School Fair, featuring the Wolcotts acting up?"

"That's a good one, Kate." Laura and I had to stop working, we were laughing so hard.

"That was a good one." The voice came out of nowhere. "A real good one." Then the body that went with the voice appeared from behind the tree.

"I finally found you," Freddy Wolcott said in a quiet voice. "And you're going to pay for being so funny."

73

Everything around the tree was suddenly quiet, as if someone had yelled, "FREEZE!"

Laura was sitting with her back as straight as a ruler, one hand holding sandpaper over the hand that held the hummingbird. I was still leaning against the tree, the point of Gramps's knife touching Laura's chunk of sparrow wood. Freddy was standing over me, all hunched up, his arms ending in fists.

"I am going to hurt you where it will hurt the most, Hayseed."

"And just where is that, Wolcott?" Laura asked.

I stared at her. She was on her feet, glaring Freddy in the eye. You could tell no one had ever talked back to him. For a moment he seemed caught off guard, but he recovered.

"You'll find out soon enough, Laura-girl, because I'm out to get you, too. Nobody needs funny, funny people like you two."

"There goes the bell!" I jumped up. I'd never been so happy to hear that sound. "End of round one."

"Wait till round two, Hayseed. Just wait." Freddy jerked his back away from us and headed for the school yard.

11

Laura and I reached the end of the line just as it was snaking its way into school. Freddy was staring straight ahead as he walked in line. He had a smirk a mile wide. I didn't like it one bit.

"Whatever happened to the old Freddy we knew and loved?" Laura whispered to me.

"You mean the one who jabbed, fought, and yelled out in line?" I whispered back. "Where are the good old days?"

"Look at him," she said out of the corner of her mouth. "He looks as if he is about to explode."

Miss Applegate stood at our classroom door, smiling, but hurrying us in. "Let's settle down fast, everyone. We have something important to do."

When we sat down, Freddy raised his hand. This had to be a first. I looked across to Laura and read her lips — a round *o* twice. Oh, oh.

"Hold your thought, Freddy," said Miss Applegate. "We're due in the auditorium in five minutes for the assembly on the School Fair."

"But this is important, Miss Applegate." Freddy was sitting at his desk looking like Boy Scout of the Year. "Kate Gormley and Laura Davenport have been leaving the school yard every day for the past three weeks. I found them today over on the nursery school playground. And that's not all, Miss Applegate. They were playing with knives!"

"They could get suspended for that!" Juanita's voice was as high as a police siren. "Those are two of the most important school rules we have, Miss Applegate. When Mr. Ferguson finds out, he'll really go hyper."

So that was it. Freddy Wolcott promised to get me where it would hurt the most. And he did. I looked across at Laura again, but she wasn't much comfort. She looked pale, really pale.

"Freddy, quit making up stories and picking on people." This was the first time I'd seen Miss Applegate get angry with the Wolcotts.

"Ask them about it, then," Freddy insisted. "If they're honest, they'll tell you. Go ahead. Ask them."

"Kate? Laura? What about it?" Miss Applegate looked over at both of us.

Before we had a chance to answer, Mr. Ferguson's voice broke in over the intercom.

"Girls and boys, we will start off our afternoon with an assembly that I think you will enjoy. Four of our classes will share plans for their booths at the School Fair. In a few days we will hear from the remaining classes in a second assembly. I will see you in the auditorium in a few minutes."

All during the announcement, Miss Applegate was looking at Laura and me. I wanted to crawl through the floor.

"We will handle this situation later," she said when the intercom clicked off. "Right now, line up. When we get to the assembly, listen carefully to the projects the classes are presenting. In three days we are due to make our own presentation, so please be thinking."

"Three days!" Carl said as he got in line. "We'll never make it!"

"Of course we will," Miss Applegate said. "We have a great deal of talent in this class."

"That's one thing nobody's ever accused us of." Juanita laughed her loud hyena laugh. "What kind of talent are you talking about, Miss Applegate?"

Freddy stopped glaring at me long enough to give his sister the evil eye.

"I know there is talent in this classroom, Juanita," Miss Applegate said. "I know that just from working with each of you day after day. And after the assembly today, we're going to find out just what those many talents are." Miss Applegate led us into the hallway.

She seemed so definite, no one said another word. I slowed down so that Laura and I could be partners at the end of the line.

"So that's his game," Laura said through her teeth. "To get us suspended."

"He can't do that, can he?" I asked.

"Oh, yes, he can. Juanita is right for once. Mr. Ferguson is really strict about leaving the grade-school playground, and worse about bringing knives to school." Laura sounded scared.

"Even if a person doesn't know those rules?" I felt shaky all over. "How am I expected to know about that part of the playground being off-limits? Besides, I've been working with a pocketknife since I was five years old, so I didn't expect there would be a law against it."

"You wouldn't know those rules because you're new to the school," Laura said. "But I do. I know both of those rules, by heart. But when I found you there, I didn't think it was wrong to try to get away from D.D.T."

Our class was the last one in the auditorium. We were stuck in the very back, and it was practically impossible to see or to hear. But I didn't care. I was too scared about what could come after the assembly.

Mr. Ferguson was on the stage introducing some woman. "That's Mrs. Wallace, president of the Park Street Merchants' Association this year," Laura whispered. "She owns the shoe store on Upper Park Street."

"How do you know that?" I whispered back. I was amazed that Laura could think of anything but our problem.

"Because that's where I get all my shoes. Shh! I want to hear what she's saying about the booths," Laura said.

"Laura, how can you care about anything but the trouble we're in?"

"I'm trying to take my mind off it. Shh," Laura said again.

"We neighborhood merchants look forward to this annual school project, boys and girls," Mrs. Wallace said. "We hope some of you will grow up to have businesses of your own in this community. We want to give you a chance to try running a small business in the form of your own booth, and we will be watching how you manage your business operation. That is how we will judge the best booth. Good luck to each and every class."

Everyone clapped, and Mrs. Wallace sat down.

"And don't forget the first prize," said Mr. Ferguson as he returned to the microphone, holding a tall gold trophy. "The winning class receives this trophy, plus a free day at Kings Island, all expenses paid by the Park Street Merchants' Association."

More applause, and then Mr. Ferguson introduced representatives from four classes.

I had to strain to hear the little second-grade boy who got up and told us how his class was going to make fudge.

"We should have thought of something neat like that," said Laura, licking her lips.

"Laura, do you think Miss Applegate will take us to the office when this is over?"

"Oh, quiet down, Kate! I can't concentrate. I want to hear what my brother's class is going to do."

I forced myself to listen. They were going to have a portrait booth, and one of the mothers had agreed to draw portraits while the kids in the class collected the fees.

"That isn't fair." Laura frowned. "They aren't doing it themselves. The parents are running the booth. They should be disqualified." She jabbed me with her elbow. "Don't you think so?"

"I'll tell you what I think," I said, jabbing her back. "I think I'd like to be out of here and under our tree whittling and sanding." I was so depressed, I slumped down in my seat.

Suddenly Laura turned to stare at me. "I'm beginning to agree with our teacher." She said it slowly as if she had just been struck by lightning. "Miss Applegate is right. We are going to come up with a winning booth."

"What made you change your mind all of a sudden?" I asked.

"Never mind," Laura answered, grinning. "I just know we're going to win, so trust me."

Up on the stage the little first-grade representative talked about the cookie booth they were going to have. And the fourth-grade representative announced that his class was going to sponsor an apple-dunking booth.

"They did that last year, when they were in third grade," Juanita said to Freddy in her shrill whisper.

"They should do everybody a favor this year and try dunking their heads, for a change," Freddy said.

At the end of the assembly, Mr. Ferguson gave a final pep talk, and our class was the first to be dismissed. I dragged my feet all the way back to the room, fearing what we had to face when we got there. And sure enough, no sooner had we all sat down, when old Freddy's hand shot straight up in the air.

"Don't worry, Freddy," Miss Applegate said. "I haven't forgotten."

I couldn't look up. I hated that sound in a grown-up's voice, especially someone I liked.

"Kate," says Miss Applegate, "what's your side of the story?"

My tongue was glued to the roof of my mouth, and I felt my face getting beet-red. But worst of all, I was all set to cry. I clamped my eyes shut and didn't look up.

"Let me tell you what happened," Laura suddenly said. She was talking so loudly, she might as well have been in the auditorium addressing the entire school.

"OK, Laura," Miss Applegate said, "let's hear it."

"Kate started going over to the nursery-school yard the first day she came. She was new here, and she didn't know the school rules."

"Is that true, Kate?" I could feel Miss Applegate looking at me. Worst of all, I could feel a whole bunch of eyes staring holes through my head. I had just enough strength to shake my head up and down.

"And if you want to know why she was over

there, I can tell you all about that, too." Laura sounded like a trial lawyer facing a jury. "She went off by herself because some people in this class, me included, were treating her like dirt."

"But, what about the knife?" Miss Applegate asked softly.

"Yeah, that's what I want to know," Freddy said.

"Me, too," Juanita piped up.

"You Wolcotts want to know about knives?" Laura hissed. "I'll show you both something about knives." Laura pushed away from her desk and moved toward me. "Quick, Kate. Hand me your lunch box."

Since I was still glued to my desk like some kind of statue, Laura shoved me over and reached under my chair for my lunch box.

When Laura opened it, I could hear the wood pieces come klunking out. Then I heard sounds all around me, like some kind of choir singing a strange harmony of oohs and aahs.

"Why, Kate!" said Miss Applegate. "Do you mean to tell me that you did these here at school?"

"During lunchtime, under the tree right over there in the nursery-school yard," Laura said in an important voice.

But over the ooh-aah choir voices I heard old Freddy's mad voice. "So! Big deal. Gormley still broke two school rules, and she should get suspended."

"If me or Freddy did either one of those things, we'd be out of this dumb place in a second," Juanita shouted.

"That is where you are wrong, Juanita," said Miss Applegate. "We are all very fair around here, and no one gets suspended for a first offense."

"Except the Wolcotts," Freddy said with a growl.

"Freddy Wolcott, you did your first offense so long ago," said Laura, "that you probably can't even remember it."

"That's enough, Laura," said Miss Applegate. "I will handle this in my own way. Thank you for showing us Kate's carvings. They are amazing."

"I think they're amazing enough to be part of our booth for the Fair," said Laura. "And I know how to do the sanding, so I can show other people how to do it, too."

My eyes popped open on their own, and I stared at Laura like she was out of her mind.

"That's very good, Laura," said Miss Applegate. "Is anyone interested in that idea for our booth?"

"I wouldn't mind learning how to sand wood carvings," said Josephine, the most quiet girl in the room. "It just doesn't look that hard."

"Maybe we could do lots of different things," Carl piped up from the back of the room. "I make model airplanes that we could sell."

"I've got three pot-holder looms at home," Evie Langhorst said. "I could bring them to school, and teach anybody how to weave pot holders. It's really easy to learn."

"We could get a good price on those, too," Carl said.

All of a sudden, everyone was talking at once. Miss Applegate didn't try to stop us. She was too busy writing things down on the chalkboard.

She was putting down the names of people in our class, the things they could do, and under their names, the names of people who wanted to learn how to do certain things.

"I'll make candles with Nancy," said her best friend, Julie.

"I'll do model airplanes with Carl," said the boy across from Laura.

"Me, too," James called out.

"My mother could help us make a quilt that we could raffle off at the Fair," Mary Lee said.

Five girls and two boys raised their hands, and Miss Applegate scribbled their names on the chalkboard fast.

"OK, everyone. That is enough thinking for today," she said. "The dismissal bell is about to ring. Let's take a quick look at the board and at all the planning that has gone on."

"It looks like we've got ourselves a booth," said Carl.

"I agree," said Miss Applegate, pointing to all the names. "This represents a lot of talent, and our booth at the School Fair is going to show off all of it. Are there any more questions before we dismiss?"

"Yeah." It was Freddy on at full volume, and suddenly everybody went dead quiet and turned his way.

"No one is getting suspended today, Freddy, if that is what you were going to ask," Miss Applegate said. "In fact, I am glad you found out what Kate and Laura were up to. Otherwise, we would still be trying to figure out our booth."

"When do we start, Miss Applegate?" Evie Langhorst asked.

"Right away," she said. "We start tomorrow."

12

Miss Applegate was right. We did get started the next day. Now two weeks have gone by, and we're really on a roll.

It didn't all happen at once. The people who knew what they wanted to do started right away. Some others hung back, not knowing what they wanted, but, little by little, people joined up to make the quilt or pot holders, model airplanes or candles. Pretty soon, all but five were working on one of the projects.

"We will be working on our booth three periods each week up until the time of the Fair," Miss Applegate said. "I don't care what you do, but you must choose a project."

"I still can't decide," said Elaine Fields.

"Nothing looks good to me," Donald Swenty said.

"Then you have other options," Miss Applegate said. "You may think up your own project, or you may want to join me in one of mine."

"Like what?" said Bobby Thomas.

"I thought you would never ask." Miss Applegate laughed. "Pardon me while I brag, but I have a terrific green thumb. And I am also very interested in genealogy."

"What's a green thumb?" Bobby asked.

"You don't know what a green thumb is?" Elaine stared at him. "That's someone who is good with plants. I'll sign up for that."

"Me, too," Donald Swenty said.

"I guess I will, too." Bobby did not sound too happy. "What do plants have to do with our booth at the Fair?"

"I can show you how to make cuttings from my jade plants," said Miss Applegate, "and we will sell our newly potted plants."

"What's that other mumbo-jumbo thing?" Freddy called out from the back of the room.

"Genealogy, Freddy. It is the study of family ancestors. Finding out about your family roots could be your project."

"No project for me," Freddy said, folding his arms across his chest.

"Everyone will be involved, Freddy, because this booth is our social studies unit for the quarter."

"I don't see social studies going on here with

people hacking away with knives and slinging some dirt into pots for dumb plants. If that's social studies, I'm on the wrong planet."

"You are on planet Earth, Freddy, where learning to set up your own business is very much a part of social studies. Many people, like our merchants in the Park Street Association, make their living by running their own businesses. And that is what this project, which we will be doing for the next quarter, is all about. So decide what part you will have in our booth at the Fair."

"No part."

Miss Applegate wasn't about to let him get away with that. "Freddy, fifth graders study social studies in school. It is the law on planet Earth. I will have your decision by the time school is out today."

"What about me?" Juanita Wolcott piped up in her squeaky voice.

"The law includes you, too, Juanita. You have many choices. What is your decision?"

Juanita looked slowly all around the room at each table where projects were going on. All of a sudden, her eyes stopped at our table. I tried to scrunch myself together so that she wouldn't see me, but it didn't do any good. She was looking at me, all right.

"If I brought my knife to school," she said, staring a hole straight through me, "I would probably get kicked out in a minute."

"You have made your choice then," said Miss Applegate, ignoring her remark. "You will work with the carving group."

"Don't you go rolling your eyes at me, Laura-girl," Juanita said as she pulled up a chair between Josephine and Laura. "I know more about working with a knife than you know about breathing."

Laura opened her mouth to say something, but closed it when she saw Miss Applegate coming toward us.

"We have plenty of wood, Juanita," she said, "and I brought three different kinds of knives, so take your pick."

"I've got my own knife."

"Good enough," said Miss Applegate, just as cool as could be. "Choose your piece of wood today, and bring in your knife tomorrow."

I looked over at Laura, and I knew what she was thinking. Up until now, we had either ignored Juanita Wolcott, or we had fought back at her as best we could. Now, we were all going to have to work together and be halfway decent.

"Here goes," I said under my breath.

"What did you say?" Juanita said, looking over at me and narrowing her eyes into two little blue slits.

"What kind of knife have you got?" I cleared my throat, acting like I was repeating what I had just said.

"It's Swiss, the best one they make," she said, glaring at Gramps's knife like it was dirt.

"Sounds good." I couldn't think of anything mean and nasty to say back.

Juanita looked so surprised, she didn't answer. Suddenly something important dawned on me. The only way to live through these next few weeks with Juanita Wolcott was to play it cool, just like Miss Applegate did. Ignore 99 and 99/100% of everything she did and said, take what was left and go with it. Just realizing that got me through the first period. As we lined up that afternoon for dismissal, I heard Miss Applegate tell Freddy to stay after school and let her know his decision.

"Freddy is doing the genealogy thing," Juanita said the next day after she flashed her Swiss knife around the table for everybody to see. I guess she decided to say something civilized for a change, since we all agreed her knife was very good.

I sneaked a look over at Freddy. He sat at a table surrounded by books, charts, papers, pencils, rulers, and Miss Applegate.

"He doesn't look too happy," Laura said.

"He's not." Juanita was studying my hummingbird. Then she poked a hole into her own chunk of wood. "But Miss Applegate got him after school and did a sell job about genealogy. She told him how much fun he would have finding out about our ancestors."

"I wonder how genealogy is going to be part of our booth at the Fair," I said.

"Maybe Freddy is going to sell copies of your family tree to show people how it's done," Laura said. She rolled her eyes over my way and crossed them when Juanita wasn't looking.

"That's a laugh. What family tree?" Juanita snorted. "We got a mother and a grandmother, period. Miss Applegate is in for a big surprise if she thinks Freddy is going to dig up ancestors. And she's in for an even bigger surprise if she thinks I'm gonna carve anything more than my initials on tree trunks. That's the only reason I even got my knife in the first place."

"With a good knife like that, you could do a lot more than carve your initials in trees, Juanita," I said.

"No way," Juanita said, eyeing my hummingbird. "Miss Applegate can forget about the Wolcotts winning a prize for this dumb class."

It was one of the few times I agreed with Juanita.

13

After a few days Freddy was finding out some things about his family, and Juanita was catching on to carving something besides her initials. At first I couldn't figure out how she was learning to whittle so fast, because she sure wasn't asking me for any advice. But then I caught her watching me out of the corner of her eye when I did certain things with Gramps's knife.

"I don't know what you are carving," Laura said one afternoon, looking over at Juanita, "but it sure is looking good. Real good."

"I told you I knew how to work with a knife." Juanita gave Laura one of her smug looks.

"Well, pardon me," Laura said.

"It does look good," I broke in fast. "It's a great-looking fish. What kind?"

"Carp, since I also happen to know about all kinds of fish, too. So there."

Without looking over, I could read Laura's mind. She was telling me to forget Juanita. Who needs a Wolcott, she was saying.

"So I guess you know how to fish, too," I said before I could stop myself.

"Yeah."

"Where do you fish around here?" I asked.

"Down on the river."

"Whereabouts?"

"The Public Landing down from the Serpentine Wall," Juanita mumbled.

"What kind of bait?"

"Night crawlers, mostly."

"What else do you catch besides carp?"

"Some catfish, now and then." Juanita stopped carving and looked at me. "You fish?" she asked.

"Back home I do."

"Do you miss it?"

"Sure do."

There was a long pause, while I saw Juanita looking at me.

"Do you know where the Public Landing is?" she blurted out.

"No. I don't know much about the city at all," I answered.

"You don't have to know much about Cincinnati to know where the Public Landing is." Juanita said it in a disgusted voice. She put down her knife. "It's a twenty-minute walk from Bonehead's Store. Here, give me a sheet of paper. I'll draw you a map."

I pushed my notebook toward her.

"Here's my pencil," Laura said when she finally got her mouth back into working order again.

"Thanks." Juanita took the pencil and started making lines up, down, and across the paper.

"Here," she said, pushing my notebook back at me. "Where I put the X is the best place for carp."

"Thanks," I mumbled in response. I was afraid I would spoil everything if I said another word.

Juanita started to pick up her knife again, but something across the room caught her eye.

"Hey, what's Bobby Thomas bugging Freddy about?"

Laura and I both turned our heads at the same time. Sure enough, Bobby was leaning across the table from Freddy, trying to read upside-down what Freddy was writing. He was close enough to Freddy Wolcott to get a big punch in the nose.

"Clear out of here, Thomas," Freddy snarled. "Get back over there where you belong. Over there by the sweet little jade plants. Can't you see I'm busy?"

"I don't like getting my hands in all that dumb dirt," Bobby said. "I think I want to switch to this genealogy stuff you're doing."

"No way!" Freddy said, hunching over his papers and books so Bobby couldn't see. "I'm working on this by myself."

"Says who?" Miss Applegate had picked up their talk from clear across the room where she was helping Donald and Elaine repot jade plants. She wiped her hands on her apron and walked over.

"What do you want to know, Bobby?"

"I just want to see what the genealogy thing is all about," Bobby said.

"Freddy is making different kinds of family trees and charts for people to buy at our booth. He is going to show them how to trace their ancestry."

"I wouldn't mind knowing more about my ancestors," Bobby said. "How do you do it?"

"You're in luck, Bobby," Miss Applegate said. "Freddy has been learning all of the possible sources for research. He needs to practice on someone."

"No! I want to do this genealogy thing alone." Freddy threw his pencil down. "There's no way I'm giving out any information to Bobby Thomas, and that's final."

"Freddy, you are going to share the genealogy

information I shared with you," said Miss Applegate. "That is the way we all learn. And *that's* final."

"Maybe he doesn't understand how it all works, and maybe that's why he doesn't want to do it," said Bobby, trying to be helpful. "I know sometimes that happens to me."

"What do you mean, I don't understand?" Freddy snarled. "I know that both my great-grandmother's parents came from Germany in 1898. That's more than you know about your ancestors, Bobby Thomas."

"You're right, Freddy," Bobby said cheerfully. "That's true. I don't know anything about my ancestors."

"Freddy, you certainly did get that information quickly," Miss Applegate said. "Yesterday, you didn't even know your great-grandmother's last name. What happened?"

"I have my ways," said Freddy.

"Juanita," Laura leaned over and whispered, "do you know how he did it?"

"Sure." Juanita laughed.

"Tell," Laura said, moving her chair closer to Juanita's.

"It was a real shakedown," Juanita said.

"A real what?" I moved my chair closer.

"Freddy pulled a fast one on Mom," Juanita said, working her knife faster and faster along the tail of her wooden carp.

"What happened?" Laura and I both said together.

"Last night when Freddy asked Mom about her grandparents, she told him she was too busy to talk about it. So when she went out to the store, Freddy got the key to her old trunk and opened it," said Juanita.

"If I did that, I'd get killed," Laura said.

"That's just about what happened." Juanita put down her knife and her fish so that she could use both hands to tell the story. "Mom came home before Freddy was halfway through the trunk."

"Did your mom give it to him good?" Laura was smiling without realizing it.

"She was mad, and she was getting all set to warm his bottom good. Then Freddy told her that he had to know about her grandparents, or else he would flunk social studies," Juanita continued.

"So what happened?" My knife was down on the table right next to Juanita's.

"She was so surprised that Freddy cared about failing social studies, because he sure had never cared before, that she sat right down on the floor with him and started going through the pictures in the trunk. And before you knew it, she was giving him the whole lowdown on her grandparents," said Juanita.

"Like what?" I asked.

"All kinds of stuff about her grandparents and how they came here from Stuttgart, Germany. Mom said they met on the boat coming over, and they got married when they got to Cincinnati. She told all about how her grandmother used to say how tough it was coming to a new place, not knowing anybody."

"That must be rough," Laura said, looking over at me.

"The hardest part was not knowing the language," Juanita said. "She told Freddy all kinds of stuff, and he was writing dates and places down like you wouldn't believe."

"He sure got out of that one." Laura seemed let down.

"Is that what he's doing now, filling in your family tree?" I looked over at Freddy, who had his head bent down.

"Probably," Juanita said, picking up her knife and her carp. "And all I've got to say is Bobby Thomas better stay clear of Freddy."

The three of us sneaked a look over at Freddy,

who was copying information from a card he was holding. He was very busy ignoring Bobby, but Bobby didn't take the hint.

"I think genealogy is what I want to do," Bobby said. "It looks like fun. Show me what to do, Freddy. OK?"

Freddy raised his head to say something to Bobby, but Miss Applegate gave him the evil eye. So instead, Freddy made a big face, picked up a ruler, and put it and some paper down in front of Bobby.

Five minutes later the dismissal bell rang. "Already?" Bobby said in disgust. "And just when I was getting into this."

"That's exactly how I feel," Laura said, putting her sandpaper and sparrow away. "There is so much going on around here that I feel I could stay for another hour just to see how it all turns out."

"Not me," I said, hurrying to get in line. "Wednesday is my heaviest delivery night. Mr. Bono gets a ton of orders in the middle of the week."

"Quit complaining," said Juanita. "You're lucky to have a job at all. I sure wouldn't mind doing what you do." She said the last part in a whisper, but Laura and I picked it up.

"Why don't you ask around?" Laura said. "When I saw that Kate had a job, I found one, too, at Miss Silen's gift shop. Storekeepers around here are always looking for somebody part-time after school or on Saturdays."

"Yeah, that's easy for you to say, but who's going to hire a Wolcott? You tell me," said Juanita, staring at Laura like she was clear out of her mind. "You've got to know the right people to get a job around here."

"I could ask Mr. Bono about my job. We're leaving in June, and he'll need somebody to take my place. That's for sure." It was all out of my mouth before I could grab it and stuff it back down me. Suddenly, I was trying to picture Mr. Bono's face when I made that suggestion to him.

"I wouldn't mind that at all," said Juanita, looking like she was seeing me for the first time. "But I'd sure be surprised if he took you up on that idea."

Me, too, I was thinking. Then I found myself looking back at Juanita, like I was seeing her for the first time, too. She was not afraid of work, and she wasn't so bad, either, once you got used to her ways. Maybe it would work.

14

That night I wasn't really surprised to see Mr. Bono out in front of the store, looking up and down the street for me. He was doing that a lot lately.

"Little Gormley, where in the name of heaven have you been?" Mr. Bono rubbed the sweat off his face with his apron. "I thought the gypsies stole you away."

I started to explain that I came home every day at this time, but he wasn't listening.

"I've got a million orders," Mr. Bono said, "and I need you to get going fast. But, just my luck, guess what? Your mom, she wants you upstairs first because you got a letter from your grandfather."

"Great!" I started running toward the stairs.

"Please don't be mad," I told poor Mr. Bono. "I promise I'll be right down."

Mom was on the phone with Dad. She pointed

over to the kitchen table where my letter was. I tore it open. Two pictures tumbled out onto the floor. I picked them up, one in each hand. One was of Janis Barlow sitting on top of Blue Bonnet. The other was of Gramps and Grandmother standing in the front doorway, holding hands and looking pretty self-conscious about having their picture taken. I pulled the letter out of the envelope.

Dear Kate,

I guess you can figure out what happened here. Janis came over to the house one day after school with the new Polaroid camera she got for her birthday. I guess she was pretty lonesome for you, and she wanted to send you some pictures so that you could get lonesome, too. I told her I would send them to you with a reminder that you owe her a birthday letter. So, that is what I am doing right now.

We think about you every morning, Kate, when we pass that empty bedroom of yours. Your grandmother finally figured out that maybe it would help if we just closed your door so it wouldn't hurt so bad.

103

*You sit down one of these days soon
and write Janis for her birthday. And
while you're at it, why don't you put a
little something down on paper for
your grandmother and me.*

*Tell your dad to call me this Sunday
about 2:00. I need to check with him
about some hog prices. We love you
and miss you, so hurry home.*

*Love,
Gramps*

*P.S. Did you ever get to the bottom of
your trunk and find my package? I
sure would like to know.*

I wasn't crying, but I did rub my eyes a little
bit on my sleeve. Suddenly, I became aware of
Mom's conversation with Dad on the other line.

"But, Ben, that's a lot of money," she said.
"That would cost us about sixty dollars a month
for a year." There was a long pause. Mom listened
and nodded, and I tried to figure out what was
happening.

"It does sound nice," she said, "and Vic is kind
to offer to sell it to us without charging interest,

but let's not rush into anything yet. Why don't we talk it over when you get home?"

"What?" I said to Mom when she hung up.

"Your dad has a chance to buy Vic's old Ford for seven hundred dollars."

"No!" I put Gramps's letter and pictures down on the kitchen table. "No."

"What do you mean, Kate? What's wrong with you?"

"No! We don't want Vic's old broken-down car."

"It's a good buy, Kate, and it would make our life here much easier if we had a car," Mom said.

"No. No. No. We would end up *never* going back home. Ask Eliza McCracken, if you don't believe me." I was crying and choking and I couldn't stop myself.

"What is it that I should ask Eliza McCracken?" Mom came around the table and held my head against her chest, so close that I could hear her heart beating fast.

"Ask her about how everybody comes to the city long enough to shake the money tree." I was still crying.

"That is an old Kentucky expression, Kate. Do you know what it means?"

"It means you want to make a lot of money quick." My chest hurt from all the heaving I was doing. "But Eliza will tell you that once you start making money, you start buying, and then you're glued to the city like pitch to the road. That's what she says, Mom, and she says that then you have to stay away from home forever. Go ahead. Call her up and ask her. She'll tell you all about it."

"Stop your crying, Kate. Maybe I don't really have to call and ask her what she means." Mom was rocking me back and forth. "We'll talk about it tonight when you and your dad come home."

"Help, Little Gormley! How long is that letter?" Mr. Bono shouted from the foot of the stairs. "Can't you come and help me?"

"Some things never change, right, Kate?" Mom looked at me. Her eyes were wet, too, but both of us started laughing at the same time.

"Hurry back." She gave me a pat. "We'll talk tonight."

Figaro was standing at the door next to my overloaded grocery cart, and Mr. Bono was patting Figaro. "I am ashamed of myself for acting so bad, Little Gormley," he said, looking down at his feet.

"It's OK, Mr. Bono. I understand."

"You don't understand everything, Little Gormley. You don't know how much I have come to need your help."

"You mustn't feel that way, Mr. Bono. We're only going to be here until June."

"I don't want you to go. I want you to stay."

"No!" I almost yelled. "No, we can't stay. We just can't stay."

"But what will I do without you?" Mr. Bono sounded desperate. "My wife is sick. I am too old to do this by myself. What do I do without you in June, Little Gormley?"

"I've got somebody for you, Mr. Bono, and she's good," I blurted. "I'm going to get her ready to take my place." I prayed that he wouldn't ask me who it was.

"OK. OK. It's good you think of your old friend Mr. Bono, Little Gormley. We'll talk about this later. No more talk now. We'll live for right now. Here is the list. Hurry back, so your mama and I don't worry."

Mr. Bono was right. No more talk for more reasons than one. I grabbed Figaro's leash in one hand and the cart handle in the other and took off.

So much had happened since we'd arrived. When I thought about how long it used to take me to do the deliveries and how fast I could do them now, I could hardly believe it. In some funny way, I felt as though I'd lived here a long time. Almost as if I'd known Mr. Bono and Figaro all my life. Laura, too. And even the Wolcotts.

Stoob's Bakery was right ahead. I had to smile. Mr. Stoob, my friend and protector.

"How's it going, Kate?" Mr. Stoob was out front wiping down his windows. "Any new adventures with the Wolcotts?"

"There's a new adventure, all right." I pulled his grocery bag off the cart and put it on the counter inside.

"Let's hear it." Mr. Stoob followed me into the store and grabbed a cookie for me and one for Figaro off the tray. "I like to keep up with these things."

"Juanita is bringing her knife to school."

"Really." Mr. Stoob looked worried. "Why?"

"Our class is getting ready for the School Fair, and Miss Applegate got me to help Juanita whittle."

"You never told me you whittled."

"You never asked, Mr. Stoob."

"That's true. Is this the annual School Fair that the Park Street Merchants' Association sponsors?"

"That's the one."

"I am treasurer," Mr. Stoob said.

"You never told me."

"You never asked."

We both looked at each other and laughed.

"And what's Freddy doing while Juanita is operating her knife? Is he working with pistols?"

"No. Genealogy."

"Genealogy? Freddy Wolcott doing genealogy? I don't believe it."

"And he found out all about his mother's grandparents."

"Where did they come from? Alcatraz?" Mr. Stoob laughed at his own joke.

"Juanita said Freddy found out that their mother's grandparents came over from Stuttgart, Germany, in 1898. They met on the boat coming over, and were married when they got here."

"That is strange." Mr. Stoob leaned over the counter and looked at me over his glasses. "My grandparents came from the village of Fellbach, just outside of Stuttgart, in the same year. They may have been around the same age as Freddy's great-grandparents."

"Do you think they could have come on the *same boat*, Mr. Stoob?" I asked.

"Well, now, that would be something, wouldn't it, Kate?" Mr. Stoob shook his head. "Stranger things have happened, I suppose. Does Freddy know what boat his great-grandparents came over on?" he asked.

"I don't know. But the way Juanita talks, he's

really bugging his mom until he gets all the information he wants," I said.

"Tell him to drop by sometime and see me. I have a copy of all the ships and their passengers that sailed in 1898. We could probably find his great-grandparents." Mr. Stoob followed me out the door and looked at his watch. "Meanwhile, I am keeping you from making your last stop. Look up there, Kate. Eliza is standing at the window waiting for you."

I waved at Eliza, grabbed her bag of groceries, and rushed up the steps, two at a time. "Kate Gormley, I have been standing here maybe a half hour or so, waiting for you," she greeted me. "Come right in."

"Eliza, I asked Mom to call you." I blurted it out instead of a hello. She held the door open for me, and I walked past her into the kitchen and set the groceries down on her table. "Mom and Dad are thinking about buying a used car, and you've got to talk them out of it," I said.

"Kate, I don't even know your mama and your daddy. And even if I did, I wouldn't be presuming to tell them how to live their lives," Eliza said.

"But, Eliza, if you don't, then we will end up staying here forever, just like . . ."

"Just like Eliza McCracken and her family." Eliza started unloading her groceries and all the

110

time she was looking over at me and smiling. "Is that what you were going to say, Kate?"

"I'm sorry. I didn't mean to hurt your feelings."

"You're not hurting my feelings, Kate. The McCrackens had the choice of going back to Kentucky or staying here." Eliza opened the refrigerator door for me, and I put in the milk and eggs.

"And we made our choice. We stayed. And now your family is doing the same thing."

"But I want us to choose the other way, and I want you to help."

"No, Kate. I can't help. Only your family can decide. And no matter what they choose, there is really only one thing that matters."

I didn't want to hear any more, but Eliza put down the two cans she was holding and took my face in both her hands so that I had to look at her and listen.

"Happiness is not a place, Kate. Happiness is a way of looking at the things that happen to you, and turning those things into something fine. We are each in charge of making our own happiness happen. And that is what really matters, wherever you live."

I could feel Eliza's fingers brushing away some tears that I couldn't hold back.

"You remember what Eliza McCracken just told you, Kate Gormley. Now you'd best run along. It is getting dark. Most likely, your mama and your daddy are waiting on supper for you right this very minute."

She was right. We both knew there wasn't any more to say. I took Figaro's leash and moved on down Park Street with the empty cart banging against the sidewalk.

15

Park Street was quiet at this time of night. There weren't so many cars whizzing by. Most of the people who usually sat on their stoops had gone in for dinner.

It was suppertime at the farm, too. I imagined exactly what was happening. Gramps had locked up the barn, and he was moving toward the kitchen. Maybe right now he was washing up at the sink. Grandmother was pulling the skillet off the top of the stove. It was Wednesday, so she had fixed fried liver and onions and her own garden carrots in a dill sauce.

Bono's Food Market was just ahead. Fig saw the sign and started trotting. The lights were on in our apartment. Mom was probably doing up her eggplant casserole. Dad was sitting at the kitchen table, and they were talking about the car, about us. What would they decide?

"Maybe happiness isn't a place, like Eliza says,"

I told Fig. "And maybe you can create your own happiness, like Gramps says. But there is one thing for sure. It's a lot harder to be happy in some places than in others."

Much later that night, after Mom, Dad, and I had talked, and the lights were out, I sat on my bed and looked out the window. The silhouette of my poor old scrawny tree spotlighted in red and blue fluorescent lights was still there rubbing its branches against the rusty fire escape. That hadn't changed. But other things had since that night when I'd sat on this bed, turned on my flashlight, and read the note Gramps had wrapped around his knife.

I knew that tonight I owed Gramps a long letter. There was so much to tell him. Where should I start? I thought about Gramps's note.

I'd taken his advice to heart. I had whittled away with his knife, and somehow I did what Gramps said I could do. I had shaped part of my world just the way I wanted it.

My letter to Gramps couldn't wait any longer. Tonight was the night to write it.

And that's just what I did. I turned on my flashlight, and I took that pencil and poured out my heart to Gramps. I told him about the Wolcotts and the hard time they had given me and about all the ways they had hurt me. I told him how his

114

note and his knife helped me know I was the one in charge of making my own happiness. I let him know that because of him, I made my own bedroom in Cincinnati, got our class going in the School Fair project, and even made myself and Mr. Stoob and Mr. Bono change our minds (a little bit) about the Wolcotts. I let Gramps know about Miss Applegate, Laura, and Eliza McCracken, too.

Suddenly I felt tired all over, but I knew I couldn't stop until I'd written Gramps about what had happened tonight. I turned my paper over and continued.

Dad said that we'll call you on Sunday at 2:00. He'll probably tell you about the old Ford that Vic Bono offered to sell us cheap. Mom and Dad voted on whether or not to buy it. It was a tie, so I got to vote. I voted no because it would slow us down getting back home.

But I did learn one thing, Gramps. If we would have stayed here, I could have done it because of what you and Eliza McCracken have taught me. Eliza says that we are each in charge of making our own happiness happen.

And you say that people don't find
happiness, they create it. You're both
saying the same thing, using different
words. I guess that's why I feel I've
really learned something important
that's going to stick with me forever.

It's midnight, Gramps, and I am dog
tired, but I just had to tell you and
Grandmother how much I love you.
Tell Janis she's going to get her birthday letter tomorrow. And tell her
Stinky Fitz is nothing compared to
some people I have met!

Love,
Kate

P.S. Give Blue Bonnet a lump of sugar
for me.

16

I couldn't believe those next few weeks. Going to school and working at Bono's were practically full-time jobs.

I spent most of my time working on our booth at the School Fair. But I wasn't the only one. Almost everyone in our class was doing the same thing. Joan Sully's dad helped us build a wooden booth big enough to hold all of our different craft projects. Some other parents helped paint it. Laura's mom set up her portable sewing machine and taught the kids how to make red, white, and blue bunting for around the booth. We had a winner! At least we thought so.

The day after I wrote Gramps telling him about the Wolcotts, I decided I'd better pass along Mr. Stoob's genealogy message to Freddy.

"Hey, Freddy," I said, walking over to the table where he and Bobby Thomas were working on some charts, "Mr. Stoob wants you to drop by the bakery."

"What about?" Freddy didn't even look up.

"He's interested in what you're doing in genealogy, and he wants to talk to you about it."

"How come he knows what I'm doing, Gormley? And what's it to him?"

"I told Mr. Stoob," I said, trying to stay calm, "that you found out your great-grandparents came from Stuttgart, Germany. He got interested because his own grandparents came from near Stuttgart the same year."

"You got no business telling Stoob about my family, Gormley."

"Look, Freddy." Something inside me suddenly snapped. "Mr. Stoob's got lists of the people on all the ships who came over from Germany in 1898. He's got them all because that's the year his grandparents came over. When he heard that your great-grandparents came over from Germany the same year, he thought you'd like to see his lists." I could feel the red heat spreading from my face down the rest of my body. "Mr. Stoob also happens to be looking for some part-time cleaning help after school. I thought that might mean you. But just forget it. You don't deserve a favor from anybody."

"Cool down, Gormley." Freddy Wolcott had put

his charts down and was looking at me. "Has he got the lists at the bakery shop now?" he asked.

"How am I supposed to know?" Suddenly I was tired. I just wanted to go back to the whittling table and mind my own business. But it looked like nothing was going to go my way.

"Time to clean up, children," Miss Applegate called out as she looked at her watch. "Carl has just told me his idea for advertising our booth. While you put your things away, listen to him and see what you think."

"I thought we could pass out flyers for the shop owners to hang in their windows advertising all the things we're doing at our booth," Carl said, pointing to the work tables around the room. "We've got our quilt, pot holders, model airplanes, genealogy charts, and hand-carved wooden animals. I think people should know in advance what we're doing so they can bring plenty of money to buy our stuff."

"They've already got one ad in their windows about the School Fair," said Laura. "Would they bother with another one advertising just our booth?"

"It would show them we know something about advertising our product," said Carl. "And that's one of the things they're judging the booths on, isn't it?"

119

"I know for a fact that Mr. Stoob doesn't like his windows messed up with a lot of flyers," I said. "I had a hard time convincing him to tape up one flyer about the School Fair. He'll probably say no to another flyer just about our classroom booth."

"So he says no," Juanita piped up. "We should go ahead and try it with the rest of the shop owners. What've we got to lose?"

"How many agree with Juanita?" Miss Applegate counted raised hands. "The majority of you are in favor of distributing a flyer of our own," she said. "Let's do it. Who can stay after school and design one?"

Emily and Carl raised their hands. "We will run them off this afternoon when you finish the design," Miss Applegate said to them, "and we will get them to the shops by tomorrow afternoon."

By the next afternoon Miss Applegate was handing out our flyers to volunteers to deliver to merchants up and down Park Street.

"I'll take the one for Stoob's Bakery," Freddy said, looking at me out of the corner of his eye. "I've got to go and see him anyway."

I made the bakery my last stop late that afternoon. Mr. Stoob hadn't ordered any groceries, but I dropped in on him anyway. By the time I arrived, he looked like he was ready to explode with news.

"Freddy Wolcott dropped by, looking for my

ship lists, Kate, and he seemed real disappointed that I didn't have them with me," Mr. Stoob said.

"So did he bang his fists on the counter and call you names?" Even though I was dying to know everything, I was fed up with Freddy Wolcott.

"No, as a matter of fact, he perked up when I told him I'd bring all the 1898 ship lists in tomorrow, and we'd look them over for his great-grandparents' names." Mr. Stoob had a big surprised ear-to-ear grin on his face. "By golly, that boy is really into this, isn't he?"

"I guess so." I said. "What about our flyer? Did he show it to you?"

"You should have been here for the flyer part of the story." Mr. Stoob leaned on the counter, and he had the most comical look on his face that I had to smile right along with him.

"Tell me," I said.

"When I saw your flyer, I told Freddy no more flyers for me." Mr. Stoob was enjoying himself. He was going to make a long story of it, I could tell. So I leaned on the counter, too.

"No, sir, I told him. I didn't want all that tape mess on my windows," Mr. Stoob continued. "Freddy said he wasn't surprised to hear I felt that way. That's a pretty good attitude for a Wolcott, don't you think, Kate?"

"Hm-m," was all I said.

"So then I told Freddy I'd make a deal with him. He could tape up your flyer if he'd come back after the School Fair was over and clean the whole window."

"And what did he say to that?" I asked.

"He said he was good at window cleaning and every other kind of cleaning for that matter." Mr. Stoob straightened up from the counter. "And you'll never guess what he said then, Kate."

"What did he say?" Mr. Stoob was taking forever to tell what I wanted to know right now.

"He suggested I hire him part-time for all my cleaning jobs." Mr. Stoob shook his head back and forth. "Just like he was reading my mind."

"You're going to hire him?" I was sure glad I'd dropped in for this little visit.

"I told him we'd try it for a month, starting tomorrow. If he turned out to be a good worker, we'd make it permanent. And do you know what he said to that, Kate? He said I didn't have to worry about a thing because he was going to work out just fine."

"He said that?" I just stared at Mr. Stoob, and he stared back.

The next day Juanita didn't waste any time when she got to the whittling table. "Freddy got a job working at Stoob's Bakery," she said, looking right at me.

I looked across the table at Laura, and I saw she was reading my mind. Here it comes, I was thinking.

"What about old Bonehead, Kate? Did you ever talk to him about me?"

Laura bent down over the bird she was sanding while I cleared my throat. "I told Mr. Bono I had someone to replace me when we leave in June," I said.

"Did you tell him who?" Juanita wasn't going to let up until she had the answer.

"Not yet."

Juanita handed Laura her finished wooden fish to sand. "When he hears it's me, old Bonehead will say no," Juanita said. "Anybody wanna bet?"

"Why should he say no, Juanita?" Laura said. "You're a good worker, so quit betting against yourself."

Juanita looked at Laura to see if she meant it, and at me to see how I was taking Laura's conversation. She must have decided we thought she was all right. "Thanks," she said under her breath and then started on a new piece of wood.

Laura was right. Juanita was a good worker, and whatever she set her mind to do, she did. "I'll tell Mr. Bono today after school, Juanita," I said.

"Thanks, Gormley." Two thanks in a row was a record for Juanita.

"And, Juanita," I said, looking over at her, "don't call him old Bonehead anymore, OK?"

"OK," she said. "From now on, it's Mr. Bono."

"You said that just right, Juanita," I said, and she, Laura, and I laughed.

When Mr. Bono first heard it was Juanita I was offering as my replacement in June, he really carried on. "Never a Wolcott, Little Gormley," he said. "Never, never, never."

But when he heard that Mr. Stoob had decided to let Freddy Wolcott work for him, he calmed down. "Things could be worse, I guess. At least you didn't decide to stick me with that Wolcott boy, Little Gormley," he said with a big, loud sigh.

So he let Juanita come along with me for one whole week. Then I got sick with the flu, and for three days Juanita did all the deliveries herself with Figaro. Even Mr. Bono had to admit that she'd done everything just right. And besides that, none of the customers had complained about having a Wolcott deliver their groceries.

"Mr. Bono thinks you're fine, Juanita," I said when I came back to school and paid her for her three days.

"Thanks again, Kate," Juanita said, and Laura

and I didn't even exchange looks. We were beginning to get used to Juanita Wolcott acting decent.

During the next two weeks, we speeded up work on our projects. Finally the day came when Miss Applegate gave us our final instructions and said, "Children, there will be no homework tonight because of the School Fair tomorrow. Get a good night's sleep, because we will all be working very hard tomorrow."

I looked around our classroom. All the kids, even Freddy Wolcott, looked like I felt. We had thought tomorrow would never come. And now it was almost here.

17

"Wake up, Kate." Mom said. "Today is the day."

"What's the weather like?" I was afraid to open my eyes.

"It's beautiful," Mom said.

I sat up in bed and looked out. It was better than beautiful. The sun was rising over the chimneys, and there wasn't a cloud in the sky.

"Hurry, Kate," Mom said. "Don't forget your promise to Mr. Bono."

Who could forget a promise to get up at six-thirty on a Saturday morning? It was a hard thing to do, but I knew I'd never hear the end of it if I didn't offer to set up Mr. Bono's produce before I left for the whole day.

"Don't bolt your breakfast, Kitten," Dad said, touching my arm to slow it down.

"I can't help it, Dad. I have to be at school by eight."

"Why so early?" Dad asked in surprise.

"The judges are coming at nine o'clock when the School Fair officially opens. They're going to do their judging right away. We've got to be there by eight to finish setting up our booth."

"You win, Kate." Mom looked at Dad and laughed. "Go ahead and bolt."

I polished off my cereal in three swipes and was off, down the steps two at a time, and into the store.

"One thing about you, Little Gormley, you sure do move fast." Mr. Bono shook his head as he watched me lug out produce and set it up on the sidewalk.

"That's one thing I've learned since I've come to Cincinnati, Mr. Bono."

"That's not all you've learned. How about the way you've learned to deal with the Wolcotts, and then the way you taught the rest of us how to deal with the Wolcotts? Now you go along. I'll finish up. I know you've got big important things to do today."

I gave him a grateful smile and took off up the hill to the school gym.

The gym was already loaded with kids and teachers running around setting up. I had to stop just inside the door, because I wasn't prepared for what I saw. For one thing, it didn't look like

Park Lane Public's gymnasium at all. The class-room booths were placed along the four walls of the gym. A podium was set up in the center surrounded by chairs for the school band.

Ours was the longest booth and the fanciest with the red, white, and blue bunting Emily and Carl were tacking around the front of it. Bobby Thomas and Juanita were holding the big overhead sign steady, while Freddy stood on a chair and hammered it to the two support posts. As I came closer, I could hear Freddy.

"Juanita, you're going to get it if you don't hold that sign still!" Then he looked past Juanita and pulled the nails out of his mouth. "Look!" he shouted. "Here they come now. We're never going to be ready in time."

I looked over toward the gym doors. Freddy was right. Mr. Ferguson was standing there talking with the mayor and the other two judges.

"Keep cool, Freddy," Miss Applegate said. "The judges are early. We are doing fine, so just keep calm and keep hammering."

"Where is Laura with that blue tablecloth she promised to bring for the counter of our booth?" Carl was going completely hyper. "We can't put out our stuff until she comes with it."

Laura suddenly appeared, running past the judges.

"Where've you been, Laura?" Carl asked. "We've been waiting to cover the counter."

"Sorry, but I had to get Miss Silen's trash cans out for trash day." Poor Laura was hot and red. "And she wanted me to sweep up the sidewalk and street in front of her gift shop."

"I hope you did a good job," Freddy said, banging in the last nail on his sign. "Looks like she's one of the judges."

We all followed Freddy's eyes up to the podium in the center of the gym where Mr. Ferguson had led the others. The gymnasium had begun to fill up with people who were moving over toward the podium.

"Attention, everyone," Mr. Ferguson called into the microphone. "I am about to perform my first official act of our annual School Fair. I will now present our judge badges to the mayor of our fine city, to Mrs. Wallace, president of our Park Street Merchants' Association, and to Miss Silen, vice president. The judging of the booths will take place promptly at nine o'clock. That gives all of our participants approximately twenty more minutes to complete their preparations."

Laura spread her blue tablecloth across the top of the booth. And that's when Miss Applegate and the kids in our class went into action like a drill team that had been practicing for months.

Evie Langhorst and her committee hung their pot holders up and down the wooden posts on either side of our booth.

Carl's group hung model airplanes across the front of the booth.

Nancy and Julie set out their candles on one side of the counter. Juanita, Josephine, and I laid out our carved animals on the other side.

Elaine and Donald scattered their newly potted jade plants in among all the crafts.

And on the middle section of the counter, Freddy and Bobby laid out their genealogy charts.

Emily hung up the price list for all of our merchandise, and put her calculator and money box on a chair behind our booth.

Miss Applegate helped Mary Lee's group hang the raffle quilt and set up the decorated raffle box on a table next to the quilt. And Laura stood with her eyes closed, mouthing the words of her presentation speech to the judges.

"We did it, children." Miss Applegate looked at her watch. "It's nine o'clock on the nose."

"Let the festivities begin," Mr. Ferguson called out over the microphone. "The first thing on the program will be the judging of the booths. The judges will select the winning class based on the appearance of the booth, the quality of the product sold, and the advertising methods used to sell the product."

The school gym was filled with people milling around the podium and around the booths.

"Kate! We made it," Mom called as she and Dad came running toward me. "I was so afraid we were going to miss the judging."

"At this time," Mr. Ferguson continued, "we are proud to present our school band, which will perform for us while the judges make their decisions."

Suddenly, the band struck its first chord with a drum beat. Mr. Ferguson led the mayor, Mrs. Wallace, and Miss Silen down the podium steps toward the booths.

"Kitten, I want to see everything you've done." Dad put his arm around my shoulder. "Vic let me take some time to come up here, but I can't stay too long."

"And I haven't met all of your classmates, Kate." Mom waved to Miss Applegate and Laura.

Dad had to see and hear everything there was to know about our booth. And I got so involved introducing Mom to everyone that I almost forgot why we were there.

Suddenly a voice out of nowhere cut through the commotion. "Who is spokesperson for this class?" There was a sudden hush around our booth.

"I am," Laura said, using her lawyer voice. She cleared her throat. "I am very happy to tell you about our booth. When I finish, please don't hesitate to ask questions."

We all stood back while Laura came forward. I felt proud as I watched her. For a week, she had made me pretend I was all three judges while she spoke her lines. Now, as I stood there by our booth, I listened to her again. Only, this time, I really listened, the way the judges and the kids, and Miss Applegate and Mom and Dad were listening to her.

She was telling everybody how we had worked together and planned everything. How we had spent hours before and after school planning our booth and making our crafts.

I looked at our booth as though I were seeing it for the first time. A handmade quilt, model airplanes, plants, pot holders, hand-carved animals, genealogy charts. It was beautiful.

But it wasn't just the looks of the booth, or the quality of the products, or even the way the products were advertised. Those were the things the judges were looking for in a winning booth. It was much more than that. We had learned things from each other that we needed to know. And we had taught each other things that we knew especially well.

I looked over at Freddy, who was so caught up watching the judges that he almost looked like the angel of the class . . . almost . . . if you didn't know any better.

"Laura, I have one question," the mayor was asking her. "How did you advertise your products?"

"We can tell you all about how they did that." Mrs. Wallace laughed. "Every merchant on Park Street, including myself, can tell you how this class did its advertising."

"Good," said the mayor. "That's the only thing I need to know about this booth. Mrs. Wallace, you and Miss Silen can tell me all about their advertising methods as we move on to our final booth."

We watched the judges walk over to the apple dunkers' booth. We straightened things on our counter that didn't need straightening, and we talked to each other in whispers. The judges finally followed Mr. Ferguson to the podium. The band stopped when he held up his hand. The judges handed him their verdict.

"And the winner is," Mr. Ferguson said, "Miss Applegate's fifth-grade class."

Everyone around our booth was a tangle of

arms waving and clapping, legs jumping up and down, and voices screaming. Everyone was in the tangle but Freddy. He stood like a statue, holding onto the counter with one hand and onto a genealogy chart hugged tight to his chest with the other.

"I knew you were going to win." Dad hugged me and kissed the top of my head.

"Oh, Kate," Mom whispered, "wouldn't it have been grand if Gramps could have been here?"

I reached into my back jeans pocket for Gramps's knife. I thought about the magic touch.

"I think Gramps is here, Mom," I said, putting my arms around her and Dad. "I do believe he's here."

APPLE® PAPERBACKS

Pick an Apple and Polish Off Some Great Reading!

BEST-SELLING APPLE TITLES

☐ MT42975-2	The Bullies and Me Harriet Savitz	$2.75
☐ MT42709-1	Christina's Ghost Betty Ren Wright	$2.75
☐ MT41682-0	Dear Dad, Love Laurie Susan Beth Pfeffer	$2.75
☐ MT43461-6	The Dollhouse Murders Betty Ren Wright	$2.75
☐ MT42545-5	Four Month Friend Susan Clymer	$2.75
☐ MT43444-6	Ghosts Beneath Our Feet Betty Ren Wright	$2.75
☐ MT44351-8	Help! I'm a Prisoner in the Library Eth Clifford	$2.75
☐ MT43188-9	The Latchkey Kids Carol Anshaw	$2.75
☐ MT44567-7	Leah's Song Eth Clifford	$2.75
☐ MT43618-X	Me and Katie (The Pest) Ann M. Martin	$2.75
☐ MT41529-8	My Sister, The Creep Candice F. Ransom	$2.75
☐ MT42883-7	Sixth Grade Can Really Kill You Barthe DeClements	$2.75
☐ MT40409-1	Sixth Grade Secrets Louis Sachar	$2.75
☐ MT42882-9	Sixth Grade Sleepover Eve Bunting	$2.75
☐ MT41732-0	Too Many Murphys Colleen O'Shaughnessy McKenna	$2.75
☐ MT42326-6	Veronica the Show-Off Nancy K. Robinson	$2.75

Available wherever you buy books, or use this order form.

- -

Scholastic Inc., P.O. Box 7502, 2931 East McCarty Street, Jefferson City, MO 65102

Please send me the books I have checked above. I am enclosing $_____ (please add $2.00 to cover shipping and handling). Send check or money order — no cash or C.O.D.s please.

Name _____

Address _____

City_____ State/Zip _____

Please allow four to six weeks for delivery. Offer good in the U.S.A. only. Sorry, mail orders are not available to residents of Canada. Prices subject to change.

APP1090